Fastballs & Flirts
Falling For The Angels Book 4
Mika C.C.

Fastballs & Flirts
Playlist

I Like The Way You Kiss Me – Artemas

Slow It Down – Benson Boone

Selfish – Justin Timberlake

The Reminder – Chris James

Bang! – AJR

Dive – Ed Sheeran

Die With A Smile – Lady Gaga

Stay For A While – Victor Ray

Mind Over Matter – Anthony Ramos

Good Luck, Babe – Chappell Roan

Nasty Extended Version – Russ

Something Just Like This – The Chainsmokers

Love On The Brain – Rihanna

We Can't Be Friends – Ariana Grande

Let It Happen – Gracie Abrams

Heaven – Julia Michaels

MIKA C.C.

Scan To Listen!

Trigger Warnings

Mention of SA
Mention of Parental Abuse
Mention of Abuse
Mention of GA
Mention of Addiction
Mention of Death(s)

Contents

For the girls who've been looking for a tattooed & pierced biker who they just KNOW they can change.

Prologue

Jake

The hunt and chase of having found the next girl was always too good to pass up. This girl, Lexi, had barely held me down from going after the next one, but every time we went anywhere in public I felt the temptation. Her simple smile always reminded me that she wanted more. And I was– well I was trying. There were moments when I thought I could be more than just a random hook-up kind of guy, I'd been in a relationship or two before, neither lasted longer than three months. I wouldn't blame the women for our breakup, but it certainly wasn't only me. I felt the pressure of change—the pressure to put down my helmet. It felt wrong. They wanted the man they met on the motorcycle, but not the man I was.

Lexi had convinced me she was different; she was bubbly, down to try anything and didn't try to fix me, never did she try to get me to put my bike in the garage. The sweet little thing she was, might've been just too much for me. After watching our best friends slowly fall for each other, I couldn't really blame Lexi for wanting something more. Hell, I kind of did too, but I wasn't sure Lexi was it for me. We didn't argue, but we also didn't talk, we had sex and more sex, and more importantly we'd have sex with other people together. We hadn't defined what we were, so there were no problems when one of us would pick up another guy or girl at the club, but what it turned into was threesomes and foursomes.

The day Lexi and I met up at the club with Lane & Nova in tow, my brain finally did the thing. The moment I knew Nova was going to be a permanent part of my friendship with Lane. He was getting a new best friend and I was going to be pushed out.

"We can't stay." Lane said, just barely sending a look at Nova.

"Just wanted to pop in and say what's up!?" Nova yelled to me and Lexi. Lex immediately grabbed her friend's arm and pulled her to an area out of my earshot.

"My sister is supposed to be here tonight, I'm just here to introduce you guys and then we're getting out of here." Lane explained, his eyes searching the club. I've been unsure if his plan with Nova was to have a relationship or just keep hooking up with her, either way, he looked happier than I had ever seen him. A, emotion I'd never describe him as.

"Haven't I met her before? Isn't she small, annoying and crazy?" I ask, before my brain immediately wants to follow up with, 'voice of an angel, sexy and full of energy'. The way I remembered his sister was not an actual appropriate response. Normally I wouldn't give a shit, but I just kept imagining Lane never talking to me again and the thought killed me.

MIKA C.C.

The guy taught me everything I needed to know about how to get a woman to sleep with me, and that didn't include sleepovers. It's always been Lane & me taking on the clubs, finding pussy in the crowds of cleat chasers. Now he's standing in front of me, barely looking at any other woman besides Nova. Where's the guy that I used to know?

"There she is." Lane smiled, as he disappeared from my side. Nova looked at me with a reluctant smile. We've maybe exchanged a few sentences here and there, since being with Lexi, her best friend, I've been forced to be nice to her. My eyes scan Lexi and Nova as they talk for less than a minute before Lane returned with his sister.

"Kallie, you know Nova already, but this is her best friend Lexi." He says as Kallie extended a hand towards Lexi. Lexi, of course, smiled and then pulled Kallie into a hug.

"I'm a hugger." Lexi said, squeezing her tighter. The pink of Kallie's cheeks somehow manage to get darker in the already dark lighting of the bar. By the time she let go of her, the two of them smiled awkwardly at each other. I take a swig of my drink as Lane reintroduces Kallie to me for at least the fifth time.

"Jacob, right?" Kallie managed to say before Lane got a word out.

"Just Jake." I answered, trying not to smile at her. It was hard enough for me to look at her like Lane's sister when I've imagined her bent over my bike. It's even harder to keep a poker face in front of Lexi and Nova. If only I could stopped my dick from getting hard at my imagination going wild from just a glance at my best friend's sister.

"Oh, right. You're *very* particular about that. I just remembered the last time we met." Kallie's eyes narrowed, she looked away to hide the roll of her eyes, but I'm quick and not as thick as she thinks. She probably sees me as a stupid jock who doesn't pay attention to the details, so I decide to play along.

"That's right. I keep forgetting we've met before."

Kallie looks back at me with furrowed brows, almost disgusted or just plain angry that I've forgotten the times before. Like I could forget her in the red dress she wore, that dared to show her delicate ankles, exposed virgin skin that begged to be touched by ink and experienced fingers. Or the time she wore a turtle-neck under a tank top and she was so hot, beads of sweat dripped from her forehead. She pulled on the neck of her shirt, until I caught a glimpse of her throat bob as I told her that she looked nice. I'd go on with every other time I've seen the woman wear something meant to hide her perfect skin, but it wouldn't matter when Kallie would never get to know how badly I wanted to pull off those clothes and show her what my skin on her skin could do, not just to her but to me, too.

"Jake." I pulled my thoughts of Kallie away as Lexi patted my shoulder and repeated my name. I look over to Lexi who's given me all of herself, and yet I'm daydreaming about a girl I can never touch. I nodded in answer before Lexi spread her red lips, "I was thinking maybe we could have another fun night, maybe with the new girl?" She bit her bottom lip, I knew she's trying to turn me on and end our night with a bang, but adding Kallie was a no-go for me.

I don't have to look over to know that Lane and Nova have already slipped out, because Lexi only talked about our sex life as a secret to hold onto for dear life. She's not afraid to ask others to be a part of our little tryst, but we've kept it on the down low for so long that it feels like we've gotten a little too comfortable adding one more to our night out adventures.

"You ever join a threesome?" Lexi asked Kallie. My eyes grew wide as I nearly wanted to throw myself off the closest bridge. I looked at Lexi like she's crazy before my head whipped to look at Kallie and watch her reaction.

Kallie's face turned white, her blue eyes widen and her mouth opens into the perfect 'o' shape. In any of my fantasies, that shape would be perfect for my dick, but it was not one of my fantasies.

"I-uh-I..." She stuttered, "N-no. Thank you for the consideration, but no thank you." Kallie answered before she ran off. Watching her face and the way she spoke was enough to know that she was completely uninterested and blindsided by Lexi's question. I don't blame her running off after that. My eyes fell back on Lexi and her lips split into a sinful smile.

"That didn't go your way, did it?"

"Sometimes you have to scare them away to have them realize what they want." Lexi smirked as she took my drink from my hand and took a sip. "Now, do you want to get out of here or should we just fuck in the bathroom?"

"If I say the bathroom, do you promise not to do your guy voice?" I asked with a sigh.

Lexi laughed, "Oh come on, you know it was funny the first time!"

My head hung to the side, "But not the tenth time." She started to pull my hand as we walked off to the bathroom.

"Fine. I found a new standing position we haven't tried."

I shrugged, "Sure, as long as it starts with you on your knees."

Lexi bit the corner of her lips, "You really like this red lipstick, don't you?"

I smirked with a quick nod as she pulled me into a bathroom stall.

A couple days later I found the nerve to do what I'd been putting off for weeks. I don't know if it was from seeing Kallie again or perhaps the fling had run its course. The second I looked Lexi in the eyes, I felt like she already knew what was coming. It seemed to be a pretty straight-forward mutual break-up between people who could possibly be friends. If it wasn't for Lane and Nova, we wouldn't have to try to be friends. I couldn't ever get to the point of never seeing my best friend again.

Prologue

Kallie

All it took was being reintroduced to my brother's best friend for me to revert back into myself, to fall back into being the introverted girl who wore more than modest clothing. It took my brother forever to get me to go out to the club with him and his friends that night, and less than one conversation for me to run back to my apartment. My apartment hadn't really been my apartment, but Lane convinced me to live in his apartment while he moved out to live with my boss. The entire thing was awkward until he told me about his situation; he had a one night stand with her and got her pregnant. I felt like him moving in with her was taking it too seriously, but then again, my brother had two moods: be extremely serious or extremely goofy. And at least he figured out which mood was the one to be focused on after he got a girl pregnant.

I couldn't imagine what Lane would do if he knew the entire reason why I moved to Florida. He knew most of the reasons: my birth parents being extreme assholes. I blamed myself for all of my problems though, how did I know that reconnecting with my biological parents was such a bad idea? I was gullible enough to let them live in my two bedroom apartment in North Carolina, but then they started asking for favors, for money, for rides... I was fine with being helpful to them and doing what I could when I wasn't working, but it took me too long for me to realize they were using me. And even longer when I got home from a long shift and the lock to my apartment was changed. Though when I called my super to tell him that I had squatters, it only temporarily got rid of my parents. The two came back with a vengeance, and a lot of crack... They stole my car and all my money, they left drugs in my apartment and dared to call the cops on me. I'd never been sabotaged in such a personal way, but all it took was one detective to dust my apartment for prints and found my parents' fingerprints all over everything.

As the gullible idiot I was, I moved into my boyfriend's apartment but when I didn't give him what he expected from us sharing a bed, he dumped me then proceeded to kick me out. Florida was my last option; Lane was the only one who would solve my problems for me. I just happened to show up at the right time, between his problems and mine, we were like the poster children for kids who came out of the foster system. Lane and I might not have been blood-related siblings but we grew up in the same group home, and in three of the five families I lived with until I was seventeen. At one point we were a package deal, I always thought Lane had made that happen not the system. We'd been the brother-sister duo that most families wanted, until they got us. Neither of us were a problem together, but on our own–Lane was the kid who was the class jokester, always inappropriately making jokes and hiding teacher's personal items. On my own, I stayed to myself and didn't really care to socialize at school or at home. It became a problem because foster families wanted to see us kids succeed, doing extracurriculars and expecting us to do well in every subject, which I did the bare minimum to pass. But once I had graduated out of the system, things changed.

North Carolina was great for many reasons, one of them being watching the seasons change, but once I got to Florida I realized it was nothing like the state I grew up in. As I knew it, my life was changing one step at a time. From transferring from my life as a college baseball team's PR manager to an official major league PR specialist. Working with Lane's booty call turned baby mama turned fiancé, and living in a much too big apartment for one small girl like myself. Lane thought he was being a good big brother giving me his place but then he got worried about me being alone and surprised me with a dog five sizes too big for me. All dogs had eyes but this dog, Bruce, had eyes that stared at me like he knew my life was worth nothing.

I kind of believed my life was worth nothing, despite all the new changes, depression and anxiety ate at me daily, Bruce the Doberman took me on walks and I had nothing outside of work. I wanted to consider my boss my friend, but I was nervous considering she was also Lane's fiancé. I just needed someone to talk to, and she seemed to be the only one I could possibly connect with...

"Good morning, Nova." I said with a chipper voice and smile, it may as well have killed me to try to always be happy but considering I had already turned myself into the office's optimist, I was stuck with the smile on my face, Nova already looked to be in a grumpy mood, my pure opposite if we were talking just on looks alone.

I watched as Nova scratched her head and looks at me with a frown, "Morning, Kallie." She said with pause, "The wedding, you haven't RSVP'd and I assume you meant to because there's no way Lane would walk down the aisle without you there."

I chuckled, "Yes, I'll be there. I brought you the invite, but Bruce kind of ripped it up..."

"Is he getting any better with you?" Nova asked, her brown eyes looking back at me with a glint of hope.

"Um. A little. He's just very intense." I answer with a crinkle of my nose.

"Who, me?" Lane interrupted, walking into Nova's office with his friend in tow. Jake, the thorn in my side, whenever he went anywhere with Lane, he was always flirting with the girls in the office and what's worse is that he has slept with every single one of them. I've constantly heard about his sexcapades and as much as I wished I was at least a semi-normal 20-something-year old woman who has experience in the bedroom, I have zero, so hearing about one man and his ways with women just told me I made the right choice holding out. It didn't help when Jake's eyes look me up and down as he smiles at me. I had to hold back a groan and look away and just as I do I see my brother's lips meet Nova's.

I turned back around to see Jake nod towards the side, if I didn't meet him several times before, I wouldn't understand his way without words, but because I had, I knew he's nodding to get me to follow him. With heavy reluctance, I followed Jake out the door to Nova's office and closed it to give the two their privacy.

"What?" I asked in a short tone, one that I didn't know I had, but I guess Jake brings it out of me.

"I wanted to talk about the other night. At the club with Lexi– what she said was... Well it wasn't –"

"Okay, let me stop you right there," I started before my cheeks can turn red just from the memory of that night, never in my life had I been invited to become a threesome before. I was not going to lose my virginity to Jake and his girl of the week.

"We do not need to talk about that, it was embarrassing all around. Even if I was interested in a threesome it would not be with you and your girl of the week." I finished before Jake could get his thoughts out.

"Girl of the week?" He asked with a smirk, "Have you been hearing things about me, Princess?" I glared at him, I don't know when he decided to give me this nickname, but it wasn't the first time he'd used it, I only noticed that he'd never used the nickname in front of my brother, which was a good thing because Lane would murder him.

"Even if I had, it's none of your business, though I will say you sleeping around the office kind of makes you sound like a manwhore."

Jake chuckled as I see the greens of his eyes shine as he looked back at me, "I am a proud manwhore, Princess. I'm just sad that word got out before I had the chance to show you a good time myself." Now I have the chance to chuckle, because his act doesn't work on me. I thought I'd feel bad for calling him a name, but him owning it only made me dish it back at him.

"Oh, Jacob, that will never happen. Not only do I have self-respect but also, my brother would kill you if you ever tried to touch me?"

Jake shrugged, "Maybe so, but you know what they say."

"What does *who* say?" I asked confused. Jake takes a step forward and leans into me, with a whisper between his lips.

"That forbidden desires are always the most tempting." He answered as I tried not to look at his lips and the stubble that defines his chin and jawline. I bit my lip from saying something ridiculous like, *it's not tempting to a person who's never had sex.*

"That's– that's great to know, but you know what? I'm gonna get to work, since Nova's officially busy." I said almost whispering back to him. Just then the door to Nova's office opens and both of us step away from each other.

"Not me. I'm not busy." Nova said with a quick smile, her hair is completely tousled, more than it was before, letting me know that she's had some kind of quickie with my brother. I tried not to look disgusted but then of course my brother bumped into me getting out of her office.

"I think that's the quickest I've ever been." My brother's quiet voice was hardly said in a hushed tone. I gagged in response as Jake laughed at my misfortune.

"Men are gross." I groaned, "Nova, please. We were having a chat about the wedding, let's go back to that." My attempt at getting the thought of what happened in her office seemed to gather a glow in Nova's eyes. I watched her expression as she looked ready to speak, but before she gets a chance...

"You're going." Jake's voice spoke over Nova.

I quickly looked at him with a straight face, "That's funny because I thought I had to make that decision myself."

"Right, you do. It's just - I'm going and I'm the best man, so that means you have to go." I stared blankly at his response.

"I'm sorry what?"

"Oo, wait Jake –" Nova tried to speak a thought, but his finger in front of her snapped her mouth shut. My face dropped as usually no one is able to make Nova stop talking.

"Well it's customary for the best man to have a plus one–"

"Jake–" Even Lane tried to interfere.

"And if I'm being honest, I'd love to make you my date."

It's safe to say the silence between the four of us is louder than the minutes of everyone trying to talk over each other, it even feels longer. The longer I stand without a response, the longer Jake and my brother stare at me. Lane's eyes look like they're about to take on a color of red I've never seen, and when I look at Nova she looks at me curiously. But Jake. Jake is looking at me like this is a normal thing to ask me. Me. The woman who won't sleep with him, the one who gives him a hard time, and the girl that has never been on an normal date before.

Being hit upside the head would be a good way to get me to answer faster, but the longer I don't, the more my brain computes that this would be a good idea for me. That I'd experience an actual date, sure it'd be with someone I kind of disliked, but it'd be something. Not to mention, Jake is not a bad looking dude, he's just – not the kind of guy I'd give my virginity to, which is not even a big deal for a first date anyways. The words fly out of my mouth before I even consider my brother and his feelings.

"Yes." I said blinking, almost not believing I approved a date with my brother's best friend, and then Lane's face came into view. Part of my brain backtracks as I realized the mistake I may have made with the angry veins between my brother's brows and the stupid tick in his jaw.

"Only as friends." I corrected myself to repair any thoughts of harm coming from my brother's expression, I plastered on a smile as I look at him hoping the veins go away.

Jake shrugged, "That's a no-brainer. I could never get with Lane's 'sweet baby' sister."

My smile faltered, "Of course, and I could never get with my brother's sleazeball best friend."

Jake chuckled like he's got the high ground but he's no Obi-Wan. Lane looked at me with a small smile, his finger tapping the temple of his head using his version of sign language telling me he's happy I'm smart. I game him a quick thumbs up before my brother began to walk towards the locker room. My eyes revert back to Jake who's still looking at me with a chuckle under his breath.

"Jake, you coming?" My brother called from the end of the hallway. Jake turned his head to respond.

"Yeah." When Jake turned back to face me there's just a sinister smile on his face, "Looking forward to our wedding date, princess."

I rolled my eyes and faked a smile, "Can't wait." I said between clenched teeth.

Chapter 1

Kallie

Ever since my brother's wedding, things had been – normal between me and Jake. It was weird to say, but the wedding made me see Jake as a good guy, at least towards my brother. I could see why they were friends, I could see how they got along so well. And Jake, he'd been nice, I didn't even see him check out Nova's maid of honor, who I only remembered from her hanging on Jake's neck at the club. Yes, *that* girl. Whatever had happened to them didn't seem to cause any weird tension, but when she looked at me, I felt intimidated...

It'd been a week and a half since the wedding and the entire time, Nova had been on her honeymoon, which was also her taking care of the baby, so all of her work came onto my desk. I had inadvertently taken over Nova's position, and now had to handle all of her tasks on top of mine.

MIKA C.C.

My desk was a bit too small for the amount of work I had and felt like I lived in a cubicle despite having a whole floor with desks spread about with a decent sized window that looked out to the baseball field. I hated not having my own office, but I tried to work through it. I tried doing my work just about everywhere else I could before anyone had the chance to catch me. Especially, when I'd just realized I could use Nova's office for the time being. Just as I thought my cover couldn't be blown, it was...

I almost jumped, backing away from Jake as he took my headphone out of my ear.

"What'cha listening to, princess?" He smirked as he puts the air-bud in his ear. I quickly paused my music.

"Nothing you would enjoy." I said trying to get my headphone out of his ear, but he used his hand to cover it.

"Why do you have to hate me, princess?" Jake fakes a frown before his smile poked through.

"Have you ever thought I don't hate you, I just hate being called princess?" I asked as he looked at me with hooded eyes.

"Princess, princess, princess. There got it out of my system. No more princess for you. But what should I call you? Kallie is way too formal."

My brows furrowed, "Is it? You're my brother's *best friend*, I'm your best friend's sister, we should call each other by our first names, that's how it goes. *Usually.*"

"Is Kallie short for anything?"

I slapped my hands on my table, "Did you even hear anything I just said?"

"Best friend's sister, brother's best friend. I know the gist of it. Tell me."

"Kallie is short for none of *your* business."

"You're so mean to me." Jake fake frowned again, "Come on, tell me about yourself."

"Jake can't you just go back to work or something? I'm supposed to be working, not talking to you."

"Oh please, you like talking to me during work hours, it makes your day go by faster, plus you get to see my cute face."

I scratched my forehead, considering telling him that yeah his face is cute to look at, but what he's doing is sending me the wrong message. Not to mention, I am not the kind of girl that Jake would enjoy in any other setting.

"Oh my god, you're hesitating. You do like me being here!"

"Jake, do you even have an inside voice?" I asked before gesturing to the open door and the people walking past.

His smile grew wide, "Tell me how would you take me if we were alone in this office? On the floor? On the desk? Or on the couch? Or would you like it really dirty with you up against the window to watch the guys practice while I fucked you?"

My face burned hot, I don't even have to touch it to know my face is the reddest shade of pink it can get. "Please, leave!" I yelled before Jake could try and question that too. I glared as Jake placed my headphone on the desk.

"Jeez, fine." He said with his hands in the air like he's being arrested. "See you around, princess– Sorry, bad habit, *Kallie*."

Everyday at work I seemed to run into Jake, and a lot of the time I had done my best to avoid and steer clear of him. Every night I tried to be out of the office before the team to avoid walking to the garage and seeing Jake and the team walking to their respective cars. I hated walking alone in a dark parking garage but I also hated the look on Jake's stupid face when he would scare me by taking my headphone out of my ear. One of these days Jake was going to hear the music I listened to, but luckily for me I just had to tap my other earbud to stop the music. "Girly" music was a typical playlist of mine, when driving and when working out, but when I was at work and walking alone, the only music that made me feel focused and confident was not the kind of music a guy would expect a girl to listen to.

With days upon days of passing time with the little ways Jake would flirt with me, I would do my best to turn him down, but there were just days that he made it impossible. It really didn't help when he'd walk in with a tight long-sleeve that would show off his arm muscles and a backwards hat, paired with his seductive smile he would throw at every woman. I was starting to understand every woman that worked in the office; hell, even some of the men I worked with flocked to Jake. I'm sure Jake was one to take all sorts of people to bed, especially if threesomes were a normal occurrence for him.

Another night came at work and as I entered the parking garage to make my way to my car, I wasn't caught off guard by Jake. No. I was stopped by the sound of a revving engine. The sound was familiar, but I wasn't expecting to see a man on a motorcycle pass by, certainly not one with a red helmet. I had goosebumps all over my entire body when the helmeted man looked my way before he drove off. Maybe it was curiosity of who the masked man could be, but I did know one thing for sure, that night—a man on a motorcycle turned me on.

I tried to avoid the fact that I was a grown woman who had hormones and knew how the reproductive system worked since my first period, but after having boyfriends, after kissing men, I had never had that want between my legs before. I had never felt wetness in my underwear before. Now *this* was something I had to explore...

Chapter 2

Jake

Perhaps I was a little persistent on flirting with Lane's sister, but if I couldn't fuck her, I had to do something. It wasn't like me not to hit on every new woman that entered the facility yet alone worked alongside the team. The Angels were doing awesome and Nova wasn't there to do any of the work, Kallie had taken over and I wasn't going to pretend that I didn't have a little crush on her. Even with Lane's voice in my ear telling me he'd cut off my balls if I ever tried to touch his sister, nothing got me off more than Kallie bickering with me. Something about it was so - challenging and fun. I had to admit, Lane's voice was in my head every time I spoke a word to Kallie, but the payoff of Kallie flirting back told me everything I needed to know.

Flirting was fun, but I also felt bad that Kallie never seemed to talk to anyone in the office. I wanted to make her feel that she wasn't alone, so I always tried to talk to her, even if she was a busy bee with mountains of Nova's work piled up. I even tried to take a gander at some of the PR and social media stuff Kallie had to do, but none of that made a lick of sense to me. She'd been alone in Nova's office working later and later each night. Some nights I could tell she'd try to leave at a time rivaling when the team left for the night, whether it was my fault or not, I was not going to let her go by herself, even if it just meant waiting in the parking garage until she got to her car or close enough that I could slip away without her noticing.

If Kallie's social life was any indication even I had to take a step back and look at myself in the mirror. My social responsibilities had faded, since breaking up with Lexi I'd barely been at the club. Since Lane was indisposed most nights, the time to hang with the boys was limited. Even my other teammates, Ramsey, Nick and Christian, as chill as they were, they always had women waiting for them at home. Taking strip clubs and nights at the bar out of the equation, my time was spent doing what I did best. Riding. Riding my motorcycle through the city was the one thing I had that didn't automatically define me. My motorcycle didn't leave a lot of doors open for me in the dating world, it helped me realize that being alone, riding on my own is something that was just for me.

A few days after the last time I made sure Kallie made it to her car safely, I was still hung up on the thought of her seeing me and knowing it was me. The look she gave me and my bike was not something I noticed before, and I'd observed her expressions for a while. Maybe it had been a bad idea to keep an eye on her. Maybe I'd been toeing the line of the definition of stalker, but I thought I was doing right, by someone. Was it me or her, maybe some higher power? I don't know. I still couldn't get that facial expression off my mind.

MIKA C.C.

I held the line of fishing string just as Lane finished up one of his classic and yet ridiculous pranks. I tried to remember the last time he and I had set up a prank; it felt like years ago, even if it was just a few short months. The amount of time Lane was there, but not, really infuriated me. He had done everything for me to get in with this team; he had been there even before I graduated, and yet I now felt abandoned by the guy. I never thought the guy known for insane pranks would change when he knocked up our coach's daughter. I certainly didn't think it would mean he'd turn into a family man. Lane was always a toe out of line with everyone, and now he was a chill, almost boring dad. Perhaps my calling his last prank textbook, might've ignited Lane's current prank...

"And you're sure the cleaning crew will clean this all up?" I asked for the third time as I looked at the set up of Lane's prank.

"Oh yeah, I already bribed them with cake and all that good stuff." Lane replied, half paying attention as he tied the line to a spot I couldn't see with his head in the way. It wasn't until he backed up that he let out a little chuckle.

"So it's ready now?"

"Oh yeah." He patted my shoulder, "I can't believe I waited this long to prank her. It's like a rite of passage when you get hired."

I snorted, "Yeah, not wrong there. I don't think anyone else in the whole office hasn't been pranked by you."

"Exactly!" Lane smiled, "Kallie's gonna kill me but it's going to be so worth it."

"What if Nova walks into her office tomorrow and not Kallie?" I joked.

"Don't even kid about that, Nova's punch is worse than Kallie's."

8

"I didn't even know Kallie could punch."

Lane gave me a look, "The stories I could tell of Kallie getting into fights with our siblings."

I waved my hand, "Kallie? The girl who wears frilly outfits to work and chipper one hundred percent of the time?"

Lane chuckled, "Believe it or not, Jake, that girl lived in the system. We took care of each other, if I wasn't kicking some guy's ass, she was doing it herself."

I tried to huff out a laugh but something about what he said doesn't sound like a laughing matter. Why did he need to kick anyone's ass for her? Why did she have to do it, and why was violence an answer at all? I definitely didn't have the answers, I never was raised in the foster care system, but I did grow up in a neighboring city to them and knew that our schools were full of perverts and bullies.

"What are your plans for the night?" I asked, trying to drown the thought of Kallie fighting some guy off her. Did she know that what I said to her was harmless, that all of the flirting was just that?

"Ah well, Nova and I have been house hunting, so we actually have a couple places we're going to check out tonight. Oh by the way, I need to give you our realtor's number because she is one-hundred percent *your* type."

My type? "Oh yeah?" I chuckled at the thought, my type is Kallie. I mean, it's any woman that is challenging and not afraid to flirt back.

Lane looked at me and used his hands to gesture the size of his realtor's breasts and then did the same for her ass. My brows lift, definitely a woman I would fuck...

"Eh. I think I need to step back from fucking every woman I meet." The words that left my mouth caused Lane to freeze.

"Dude. for real? Did breaking things off with Lexi fuck you up? Did she say something?" Lane's questions finally sound like the best friend I once knew.

"Uh. Kinda, not really. I don't know, man. Lexi was kind of –"

"Crazy? Addicted to sex? Really annoying?"

A laugh stumbled out of my mouth, "In a way, yes. But I don't think I want to just fuck around and find out anymore. Lexi was cool to explore more of a relationship with, but she and I had different definitions of what we wanted that relationship to look like."

With Lane's hand to his chest he responded, "Wow. Dude, are you growing up?" He smirked.

"Yeah, but you try looking at all the guys on the team in relationships and tell me it didn't persuade you to get with Nova?"

There's a huff of a laugh behind his voice, "True, but the kid thing is what made it happen, not what Christian or Rams were going through. Plus, I had real feelings for her. Never thought that was going to happen."

"I don't think anyone saw that happening."

"Right." Lane sent me a wink, "Anyways. I should get going. Kallie will be here early tomorrow so if you want to get the prank on camera I'd recommend getting here on time."

A fist bump and our entire secret handshake is all we do before Lane walked off. The later it gets is when I realize I'll be blamed for the prank, especially if anyone else working late caught me. I wasn't even considering the security cameras being a problem, because when does anyone look at those?

Chapter 3

Kallie

I'm usually never the first one to open the doors to the office floor, but every once in a while the staff manager hands the task off to another manager on the floor. I'd been given the night before to lock up, but Lane had come by and asked to train late. Him I trusted with the keys and to lock up. He even delivered them to me on his way home.

I knew it was going to be a good morning because the dog didn't try to kill me when I woke up, Bruce didn't try to pull me when I walked him, and he didn't even growl the entire time I poured food into his bowl. I didn't even have a problem wearing something I never wore—jean shorts and a long sleeve shirt—the kind that kept me warm in an all-the-time very cold office.

When I went to unlock the door, I hardly looked at the lock when the key slid in, and when I pulled the key to the side, it didn't click. That's when the first alarm in my head rang. The next was the moment

MIKA C.C.

I opened the already unlocked door and walked in to hear the security alarm. Once I made it to the welcome desk, the main phone rang, I answered it to the worst news ever. The cops were on their way.

By the time the security team and the city cops made it, I had gave them the low-down of the situation. That I'd entrusted my stupid dumbass jock of a brother to lock up and he hadn't. It was a stupid mistake, but the gaze of the men in uniforms looking down on me told me they wouldn't forget how badly I fucked up. I had walked through with the cops and security all the rooms on the floor, all except Nova's. Nova's I waited for last, because that room I made sure to lock myself, but as I put my hand on the doorknob I noticed it too was unlocked. One of the cops agreed to walk in with me and as we opened the door and took the first steps in, was the moment chocolate pudding fell on top of both of us. I screamed in horror as the cop stood there with his gun drawn. What was worse was the moment I stepped toward the desk, I nearly tripped on something as white feathers catapulted onto me.

I had been turned into a dirty chicken.

And Lane was going to pay for it.

After three showers and one outfit change, I made it back to work on a mission to yell at my brother. The second I arrived, a message delivered to my phone with the video of the culprits who pulled the prank and left the doors unlocked. It wasn't just Lane; no, it was Jake too. The anger boiled my stomach, the disdain I had for Jake rose, and my heart rate went into overdrive the moment I saw him walk through the open glass doors. I watched as he turned for the coffee cart, and I made a beeline for him. I even tapped his shoulder with my finger as politely as I could without my fingernail breaking through his stupid, tight shirt.

"Hey!" Jake said with a smile.

"Hey? Hey is how you want to start this?"

"Well it's not every day that the princess comes up to me to say hello."

"I'm not a–" I groan, remembering that his nickname for me is not the reason why I'm upset. "I'm not coming to say 'hey' back." I said mocking him. Jake got a chuckle out of it which seemed like a perfect time to pull out the picture on my phone and show him.

"Oh my god!" He busted out laughing. Yeah, the picture is of me on the floor looking like a dirty chicken, with the chocolate mess all over the floor with goose feathers stuck to me as I was barely able to get up without slipping or tripping over the fishing wire.

I swipe to the next picture of him and Lane in front of my office with Lane bent over to unlock my door. "I also know it was you two idiots that set this up."

Jake had to catch his breath from his laughter before he could speak again. I wouldn't find it so attractive if he didn't push his hair back and hold onto his toned belly. I spent entirely too long checking him out before he finally inhaled to speak.

"Shit, I didn't think you'd find us out so fast."

"You two dumbasses didn't lock up! The main doors were un-locked and the security alarm was blaring! The cops had to come check everything out to make sure nothing was stolen and that I could work without being abducted or killed."

"Fuck." Jake elongated the word, "I am so sorry, Kallie." He tried to put his hand on my shoulder but I shrugged him off.

"Are you fucking kidding me? Sorry is not going to cut it; I almost lost my job!"

"Hey, I wouldn't let that happen."

"Yeah, well, good thing *Lane* can make sure that doesn't happen." I turned and stomped off, I make it to the door to the office when I feel a hand on my arm and I'm quickly turned around, backed up into the office with Jake's face crowding mine as he shut the door.

"I believe I told you, I wouldn't let that happen, Princess. Now if you want to yell at me in front of everyone, that's one thing, but running off? That's a little devil move, and you're not a little devil are you?" Jake's voice was rough as he spoke in a near whisper to me, and I feel my entire face burn, and that area in between my legs started to heat up like it did the other day. "*Are you?*" He repeated as I shook my head, "Good girl." I feel a version of want all throughout my body and I'm not sure what it entirely meant. When Jake backed away from me to give me space, I'm out of breath, but when I see his hand wrap around the doorknob is when I realized that *he's* the reason for it.

"Jake." He turned in response. "I, um. I'm sorry for yelling and storming off."

Jake turned his body further and leaned against my door with a smirk on his face, "Is that all you learned?"

The smug expression and the way Jake confidently stood there staring back at me, is definitely going to be my demise.

I should've never driven with my brother; it was just as chaotic as I remember when he got his license. Lane always drove fast, and what was worse were the times he didn't care who he was driving with. Now he was a dad, and I wasn't even sure how he was allowed to drive with a baby's life in the backseat. Maybe he only did it when his child wasn't in the car, but I was certainly scared the longer he drove.

I had confronted him more calmly than I had Jake and luckily Lane knew what to do and what to say to get the staff manager not to fire me or put me on some kind of suspension. Especially since it hadn't been my fault for trusting a jock like Lane. I loved my brother but he was really stubborn and recently forgetful as a person who had to take care of a whole other human life. I gave him the benefit of the doubt and forgave him the same way I had Jake. Except Jake was well, Jake.

Jake had been oozing sexiness since he pulled me into that office and talked to me in that low tone, I hadn't been prepared to see him exert whatever form of dominance that had been. It had gotten to the point I was having dreams of that moment, but with less clothing and his lips kissing mine. I'd only dreamt of it, knowing that's what would probably kill my brother if his driving didn't first.

"Oh shit." Lane said as he drove into the next lane, I looked over at him to see the way he looked at his rearview mirror and side mirror, before he drove into the next lane over. How many times he'd do it, I don't know.

"What's wrong?" I looked around us, the busy road was full of cars moving just as fast as him at night but nothing visibly registered as a bad thing.

"Nothing. It's just a cop."

"A cop has you jumping in your seat? I thought Nova's dad was the only one that could do that to you."

"For one, rude. Two, this isn't about me." Lane rolled down his window, "Hold the wheel steady."

I threw my head back with a single laugh, "Ha! Funny." I looked over to see him sticking his head out the window as we sped up next to the biker we saw earlier. I grabbed for the steering wheel, keeping it steady as Lane requested. My brother tapped his head repeatedly until the biker finally looked over to see him, us. Lane quickly fell back into his seat and grabbed back onto the steering wheel.

"Did we swerve?"

"Did we–Lane, you could've killed me, what was that?!"

"Did you die though? No. Sorry I was warning him about the cop." He said with a sigh.

"Him? Who? The biker? The one guy that can drive away faster than you can from the cops?"

"You need to calm down, you're being too loud about this." Lane said, not realizing he quoted a Taylor Swift song.

"Don't quote the queen to me. Who was that guy?"

"It's Jake. You know, the guy that I consider my *best* friend, the guy that's pretty much a brother to me? I know it's him because that's his signature look, the gray hoodie, the dark blue bike, the tires, the red helmet, plus he's got one of the only seats that doesn't have room for a backpack."

"I have no idea what half of that is supposed to mean, Lane. Just don't try and kill me like that again. I'd like to be in control of when I die."

Lane scoffed, "That won't happen... I really hope you can learn to let loose here, Kal. This personality of yours—it's gotten worse since the last time I was around you."

"You mean before you left me in North Carolina, by *myself*?"

"Don't guilt trip me like that." Lane said with a scoff

I chuckled, my eyes watered for a second, I blinked and they disappear, being sucked back into the vortex. "*No*, could *never* guilt trip the only family that makes it out better than anyone else."

"I wasn't responsible back then, hell, you know I'm barely passable as a dad, now. I'm just saying, it feels a lot like guilt tripping."

"You should talk, you guilt-tripped me into seeing the new Star Wars movie with you."

"It was *terrible*," we both said in unison.

"Yeah, well that was to get you out of the house for your surprise."

"Yeah, well you could've gotten us arrested for that stunt, Lane."

Lane's eyes rolled back and I smacked his shoulder.

"Hey, don't hit the driver!"

"Don't drive like an idiot!" Lane chuckled at me, but I spent the rest of the car ride home giving him an earful about his driving habits.

Since Lane had been *so sweet* to remind me that I had to let loose every once in a while, I'd made plans with Nova. Which left my brother

17

to watch his kid while we had girl time. It had been a fun day at the mall but the second we arrived back to my apartment, she noticed the box of donuts and went for it. I laughed at the crumbs that went down her shirt before we looked at the dog that took up too much space on the couch. Bruce's look of intimidation even had Nova keeping her distance from him.

"Anyways, I'm telling you, the live version is so much better. I saw it with a friend and it was SO good!" Nova said as she bit into a cronut.

"I'm sure Hamilton is good, but I was asking what we were gonna do about the team's TikTok account."

"That's what I was talking about too! We can totally do the trend of the guys dancing to this song from the Hamilton soundtrack."

"That does make more sense, but I'm just confused on how you plan to get the team to agree to it."

Nova rolled her eyes, "It's in their contract, you just gotta force them."

"But you, you are coming back to work right?"

I watched as Nova sat on the barstool and sucked in a breath, "Okay you might want to sit for this."

"No, come on! You said you weren't going to become a stay at home mom! You said you wanted to be one of those moms who worked and did cool mom stuff!" I whined back to her all the things she said to me from my first week of working with her.

"It's not that –" She bit her lip, "I'm pregnant."

My jaw dropped, "What!? Again!?"

Nova chuckled, "Yeah. And the nausea has been so much worse this time around. I know I planned to do all this stuff and to actually train you to take over my job, but I just feel awful and then I gotta get up and take care of the baby..."

"Oh my god, I am so sorry! I must've sounded so insensitive, Nova. This is so exciting, just so quick! You just had Quinn like a month ago it feels like." I said, I reached for her hands, she wrapped her hands in mine.

"Three actually. But yeah. It was super quick, but you know, me and Lane's whole relationship has been fast and I'm not really complaining anymore. Life does what it does and we just roll with it." Nova smiled with small tears running down her eyes.

"I guess that's the way to do it." I replied with a small smile. "I'm just glad you guys are happy."

"Yeah." She paused, "What about you? I feel like I've been a terrible sister in law, boss, and friend. Oh my god, I have completely abandoned you everywhere haven't I?" She groaned and I swore I heard a sob escape her as her hands covered her face.

"Oh. Oh no! I'm fine, Nova. Honestly. I'm mainly just..." I started to say as I realize, 'happy' is not the word to use with her, she'd see right through me. "I'm still a virgin." I blurted. It's not what I wanted to tell her, I wanted to tell her that I need someone to talk to, that I needed a friend but I didn't want to put all of my problems onto her of all people, especially when she's pregnant, again.

Nova removed her hands from her face as she looked at me with a shocked expression, "What? Are you serious?" The cat's out of the bag now, pussy exposed, double entendre and all.

I nodded and answered, "Yeah. I'm also not one-hundred percent sure anyone else knows though, so if we could keep this between us."

"Wait, so you're a virgin and no one knows but me?" Nova's rhetorical question didn't even phase me the way it shocked her even more. "I'm honored."

I chuckled, "well I'm glad you are, because now you know my biggest secret."

"You're twenty-four and a virgin, that has to be a record or something." Nova sighed. "So is this the kind of secret that I take to my grave, or ?"

I rolled my eyes at her, "You can't tell Lane. I'm sure he would be even ten times more protective over me if he knew that my virginity was still intact."

She points at me, "Not wrong. He said that some guy tried to hit on you at the movies and he gave him a stern look to stop the guy from even getting close to you."

"And that's part of the reason why I am still a virgin." I said, as if it's not totally my inexperience with men that does it.

"I can tell him to back off, but I know he won't when it comes to the guys on the team." At least she sounded sincere with her offer.

"It's whatever," With my head shaking I grabbed a donut from the box next to us and took a bite. "There's nothing anyone can really do to change it. Even if Lane was normal, I can barely keep a guy. Just inexperienced and not for lack of trying." I shrug with my mouthful of donut.

"That's not the right attitude though. You're miss positive, where's the girl that sees everything half-full?" Nova asked as she grabbed a new donut from the box.

I widened my eyes at her, "This is something I know, okay? I will die with my virginity and I'm okay with that."

"But orgasms are wonderful! And sex is delicious. Maybe you just need some help?"

"Help?" I asked her as I feel the crumbs fall from my mouth.

"Not from me," She put her hand to her chest, "I mean like, an open relationship maybe? I know I've had some guys teach me things in bed that I never thought I'd know about but once I did, they kinda just went on their way. They were kind of like 'sex educators'." Nova explained with air quotes, while she held her donut. "Or just find a guy friend and straight up be like 'hey I never had sex, wanna get me through that hump?" She chuckled as she shoved the donut in her mouth.

"Okay. For one, interesting. Two, not sure I needed to know those details, but three. That would be super weird for me, to ask a guy friend to help with." Not that I had any, especially not off the top of my head.

Nova shrugged, "Forget I said anything then. Just use your fingers until you die I guess."

"Huh?"

"For orgasms."

The silence between us is loud and I'm not sure if I should tell her the rest of my sexual history or if I should leave it well alone, but the longer she stared at me the more pressure I felt.

"You've never touched yourself?!" Nova yelled. Her voice nearly startled me out of my seat, but I try to make it look like I didn't just get jump-scared by her voice.

"Kallie! This is so much bigger than just your virginity!"

"It's fine. I can live without –"

21

"Oh my god, you've never experienced an orgasm to even know! Everything makes sense now."

"What do you mean?"

"Every time I bring up sex your face turns red, every time anyone has ever said anything about a food-gasm or an actual orgasm, you smile awkwardly. And every time you've experienced me or my brother right after we've had sex you look like you're going to puke."

"Now that last one is because you're having sex with my brother." I retorted.

"Oh Kallie. It's so much bigger than that. You need to find someone and fast. You've been living life without experiencing one of the best feelings in the world."

"One of the *best*?" I questioned with a brow raised.

"Yes!" Nova cried out, "It might sound stupid because we're still young, but we don't nearly enjoy this world enough no matter what age we are, and the fact that you haven't experienced this simple but amazing pleasure of this world, is so sad. And I want you to have the experience, its life-changing. And I don't mean just orgasms, sex is so profound and can open so many doors, there are so many ways to enjoy it and with whoever you're into. So it doesn't have to be a guy if that's not what you're into –."

"I'm not sure, but I think guys are."

"You have Instagram, right?" Nova asked, and pulled out her phone.

"Yeah." I answered as I show her my empty profile, my profile picture being of an emoji instead of me.

"Oh, your profile looks exactly like a bot." She chuckled as she swiped to her profile, "See the kind of pictures I post? Nothing too revealing but gives imagination to the guys that look?"

"You're married and on your second kid." I reminded her, Nova nudged me with her elbow.

"I'm showing you what you should start posting. Maybe it'll get a guy to talk to you and from there you can slowly take things to the next level. I want to see you succeed and grow. So please take this as advice or wisdom from someone who enjoys sex. You can do this, and if you need condoms I got you. Toys you'll have to buy yourself though." She finished her thought so nonchalantly that I almost took her seriously.

"Those condoms worked out real well for you didn't they?"

"Hey, it's not my fault neither of us wanted to open the box!"

I shook my head as we both laughed at how ridiculous her life is.

Chapter 4

Jake

Maybe it hadn't been such a bad idea to turn myself into a one woman guy, I didn't completely hate the idea of it when I was with Lexi. Sure, Lexi wasn't exactly the girl for me but ever since talking to Lane about it, it felt real.

Even when I woke up in bed with a woman I didn't remember bringing to bed with me. Just trying to remember the night before was hard enough. I really needed to stop drinking with the guys after an away game.

Time had evaded me the longer I tried to piece together the night before, but it didn't matter when all I kept wanting was something different than one night stands. More than a girl like Lexi. It sounded fucked up, to give Lexi a part of me, to lead her on, but I didn't feel that way toward her and I couldn't fuck it up for either of us any more than I had. I was just grateful I hadn't backslid into bed with her. Many times I had thought about it, especially with Kallie working so close to me now, the thought of having someone I couldn't have. Even if Lexi was Kallie's opposite, it would've been at least something to keep me away. My subconscious and consciousness ended it way before I knew that Kallie was going to be here for good.

Maybe it didn't have to be Lane's specific way, maybe I didn't have to come off as such a bad influence, maybe I could be a different guy. The kind of guy that brothers would want for their little sisters.

"Good morning," I hoped the smile would show my genuity toward Kallie but the expression I got back from her told me otherwise.

"It's not a good morning, not when you show up to annoy me."

I bit back my chuckle, being nice and not flirtatious was hard. "I'm not here to annoy you, I swear."

"Then why are you here at all?" She asked, the braid of her hair swayed as she turned toward me, "You should be out there." Kallie gestured to the windows that look out to the baseball field. "Practicing, playing, I don't know, somewhere, anywhere else but here."

"Right." I nodded, "I promise I will leave you alone forever, I just have two questions."

"If I listen to your ridiculous questions does that mean I have to answer them?"

"That's the hope, prin–" I caught myself and smile, "Kallie."

She looked up at me with a brow raised, I can't tell if she's impressed I caught myself or just grateful that I didn't call her by my nickname for her, "Go on with your questions then."

"First, do you think that people can change?" I watched as her brows raised and then lower into a crease, she almost looked uncomfortable.

"Hard to say," Kallie bit her lip and I had to try not to stare at the peach-hued lipstick her teeth dug into, "I don't think people can. I mean, not without some incentive. I feel like usually people change because there's something in it for them if they do. Girls change for the guy they're dating usually, kids shift into the version that makes their parents happy, and people grow into a version of themselves to get them ahead in life."

Her hard-hitting answer reminded me a lot of what Lane said, another reminder that I know little to nothing about Kallie. Heavy responses come from those who've been through the ringer, it makes me wonder what Kallie's past was like, was it family or an ex? Am I to believe that the happy-go-lucky Kallie is just a facade and that she's not the cheerful girl that dresses like she belongs in one of those elf-shows?

"Jacob."

Her use of my name snaps me out of my thoughts, the look I throw her is not the cheerful smile I had on before. I never let people use my full first name for a reason.

"Your second question?"

The corners of my lips lifted up slightly, "What would you say to us being *friends*?"

I stared as her expression changed and waited for her response.

Chapter 5

Kallie

Friends. Jake wanted to be friends with me? Had the man really given up trying to pursue me already? Was it just a trick? With my gullible personality, I'd end up having said something like *yes* just as I would discover he only wanted to get close to me to try and have sex with me. Part of me considered both sides of the answer, yes or no. I'd always been the kind of person to make pros and cons, but I couldn't really do that with him in front of me. Jake seemed to be genuinely asking, but if I were to say something like no, I'm not sure he'd take it without a fight.

"You can say no." He said almost like he's invaded my thoughts, I only assumed the question he asked first has to have some sort of connection, otherwise what was the point?

"Why?" I queried in a breath, "I mean, why do you want to be friends with me? You sleep with women and leave them on read the next day, why wouldn't you want the same from me?"

"Wow, okay, fair question, I guess."

"Am I wrong?" My brows raised.

"No, of course not."

"Thought so." I whispered under my breath.

I focused as Jake struggled to find the words, "I want to prove I'm not just known for being the playboy. I'm more than just –"

"Sex? Are you trying to say, you don't want to be sexualized anymore? Because I can promise you, you've slept with all the women, at least on this floor, so they'll never want to have sex with you after you ghosted them."

"It's not them I'm worried about." Jake stated as his brows twisted, "You know what? This was a stupid thought of mine, I'm sorry." I was taken aback by his quick change of heart, a minute too late as I observed him walk away from me.

"Wait, Jake!" I almost ran after the guy and he'd barely taken ten steps. He turns just as I reach him.

"You don't have to entertain –"

"I'll be friends with you." I said over his words.

"What?"

"I'll be friends with you." I repeated, "Friends are rare these days, so if you still want to be friends, I accept."

I watched as the smile on Jake's face grew as his cheeks met his eyes and his blue eyes glowed in the hooded darkness between his brows and cheeks. Maybe being Jake's friend can be useful to me in a way I don't know yet.

"Was there ever a time you didn't like pizza?"

"For one, that's such a weird specific question, and two, yes." I answer with the phone to my ear. It had been two weeks since Jake and I started our friendship and it had been a good start. We exchanged numbers, we talked at work without getting on each other's nerves and now we were calling each other with weird questions. Soon we'd be texting each other like Nova and I did, but for now I was okay with hearing Jake's voice over the phone.

"Was it when you transitioned from middle school to high school?"

"Oh my god, yes! How did you know?"

"I swear, the schools put something in our water that year, or something in the bread that made me hate it. It was so bad, I couldn't eat school pizzas or bagels for like six months."

I laugh, "Now that you mention it, I think that was when North Carolina had that serious drought, so that sounds about right."

"See, I thought that was just me, because I was the only one not eating wheat products back then."

"Maybe you were just a weirdo." I retort back with a smile on my face, knowing he can't see to know how easy he's made this friendship thing.

"You're right, captain of the baseball team and the school weirdo."

I snorted, "Yep definitely sounds like you." Just imagining Jake in high school jock, lanky, out of shape and with a bowl haircut, while wearing a letterman jacket was just a sight yet to be seen. He'd shared a picture of himself from his last year of middle school with the haircut and I laughed so hard I nearly dropped my phone.

"Where are you? It sounds echoey."

I had already spent a half an hour on my eye makeup but now that I was done, I had moved into the bathroom to touch up any areas I missed when applying my bronzer. As industrial the apartment felt the lighting felt like it was from the twentieth century, no LED lights in sight. The bathroom had been the only room with the brightest light. I had usually done all of my makeup in front of my phone as close to the window as possible to get the most natural lighting, but now that the sun had set I had to use the next best thing.

"The bathroom. I'm finishing getting ready for this date Nova set me up on."

"Right, because you needed help finding a date? I'm still really confused on why you'd ask Nova who was notorious for being the female version of me before she met Lane."

"It's not like I have so many friends to ask for one. And two, she made it seem like he was a really chill guy."

"Chill, hm?" Jake's voice almost sounds distorted. I don't give him a second thought as I finish blending my face for the tenth time.

"Okay, I'm done. And he should be here any minute to pick me up."

"Whatever you do, don't tell him about your special editions of Twilight."

I giggle, "I'll try not to. Don't be dumb and go to the bar. Remember your rule for trying to not be a manwhore."

"I promise not to get intoxicated and copulate." We both say synonymously. I'm not sure the wording was right, but it rhymed and made for good wordplay.

"Let me know how the date goes, just leave out the sex, I guess." Jake chuckles. I still hadn't told him my secret, especially since our friendship was new and definitely not the time when I was starting to date.

I had dated before, I was in two relationships in North Carolina. One with a high school boyfriend, which ended three months after he tried to get in my pants. And then with my college boyfriend, he was so nice and caring at first I thought it would work out, but then when kissing got boring for him, he started demanding other parts of my body that I refused to give him any part of. And the ending of that relationship still goes through my head almost daily. I should've known it would end the way it did and I definitely should've seen the signs.

After I hung up with Jake, my date showed up and while I expected a tall handsome man, I did not expect his head to be at the same level as my breasts. Once he had taken me to dinner he did not stop overcompensating by talking about the firm he worked for, or the fact that he was one of six lawyers that worked for our major league baseball team. It made sense that Nova 'knew' him. When dinner had ended, I asked to be taken home and he politely walked me to my door, then leaned in for a kiss. I let him kiss my cheek and quickly let myself inside. Hoping that not all dates will be as bad as the first.

Chapter 6

Jake

The last five weeks with Kallie as my friend had felt more wholesome and respectful than the five months before she showed up in my life. It felt like an episode out of the Twilight Zone only longer and with less sexual tension. Having a friend that was a female was nice, but sex with a female was better and the more I actually hung out with Kallie, the more I wanted to see. Perhaps it was my pact of no booze and no sex, but I enjoyed Kallie's company. What was worse about being her male friend was knowing she was flirty, sexy and with a personality I had just recently discovered and yet I had to sit back and watch her date. Being a guy friend meant listening to your friends problems, offering solutions but not expecting them to take it. Kallie had gotten notorious for telling me about her dates, but when I'd give her advice she'd come back having not used it at all. Whether it was all women or just Kallie, I finally understood Hayes when he told me the friendship between him and his now wife almost destroyed them.

It came the day that I finally had a day off at the same time that Kallie did as well; it was rare with the team being back and forth between games, but it had finally settled down where we had a little break. Despite my attempt to sleep the weekend away, I had this urge to text Kallie. It was like I was addicted to her without my dick being inside her. An occurrence that never happened. Not to me at least.

By the time half the day had slipped away, the most idiotic but possibly brilliant idea came to mind, and all it took was a couple texts back and forth, and then me and my motorcycle were off on an adventure.

"Jake, you actually made it!" Kallie said, sounding out of breath when she answered her front door.

My brows furrowed as I looked at her tousled hair, "Did I come at a bad time?"

"What? No. Of course not." Though the breath she blew out of her mouth told me otherwise. "Well..." She extended the door open and I saw what must've caused her frantic behavior. Remains of a blanket and what looked like a goose-feather pillow had covered her front and living room floor.

"What happened here?" I asked before she gave me the go ahead to come in. I took two steps as she closed the door behind me and brushed the hair out of her face when she made it back in front of me.

"Apparently Bruce doesn't like it when pillows are on the couch." She sighed with a shrug, before she started trying to clean up the mess. "Bruce gets what he wants because he's – well Bruce. He also doesn't like the dinner I've been making lately, so now he's been finding ways to throw bowls across the room." Kallie paused as she looked up to show me where there's a stain of food on her kitchen cupboard.

"I feel like I'm missing something. I don't remember you having a roommate?"

Kallie chuckled, "Oh yeah. He is the biggest, hairiest, rudest roommate anyone could ever have. Did I mention we went on a walk after our call the other day and he ran so fast by the time we got down the stairs that I fell on my wrists?" She pulled up the sleeves on her shirt to show me the scrapes and bruises.

I nearly lunged forward and grabbed her wrists, "Where is this Bruce? I'll fucking kill him."

Kallie cackled like it's nothing, "Relax, no one is killing Bruce. You want to meet him, though?"

I blew out a breath of anger for her for not taking it seriously, "Yeah, I do." She walked to the bathroom door and opened it and what came barreling out was the tallest and darkest Dobermann I've ever seen. I took two steps back but not before Kallie called out my name. I had no idea if she said it to protect myself or so I didn't hurt the dog, but then Kallie came running over to grab on the dog's collar.

"Bruce! You can't just run up on people!" She pulled on the dog's collar but the Dobermann did not move from his spot of intimidation. I surveyed him as he stood as still as possible while his head was busy sniffing my junk. I was afraid if I'd move he'd bite my dick off.

"This - is Bruce?!" It finally hit me in the face, all the stories she just told me about Bruce made more sense.

"Yeah, what'd you think you were gonna get when I said I'd get Bruce for you?"

"I don't know, a hairy buff guy?"

Kallie smiled, "Aww that's cute, you were gonna rescue me from my big angry roommate." She chuckled, "Bruce would tear your face off."

"No shit! Now get him off my dick!"

"I'm afraid it's not possible. He never listens to me and he's too big for me to move, and if he growls at me then I have to give him the room."

"Why the fuck would you take home a dog like this?" I asked, trying not to sound too panicked by the fact that this dog could indeed be stronger than me and take me out.

"That's funny, because I totally said, you know what I need, a huge dog that I can barely take care of myself that will run my life when I'm home and protect me from any strangers, including myself." Kallie gave me a tight smile.

"Lane fucking did this didn't he?"

"Overprotective big brother bullshit, I guess." She shrugged as she dropped Bruce's collar and stepped away from me. "Want a water?"

I nodded before I spoke, "So I'm just forced to stand here waiting for Bruce to make a move?"

"Pretty much," Kallie answered with her back to me as she brought me a bottle of water from her fridge.

"Does he have any treats?" I asked as Bruce looked up at me, his head cocked to the side and that was when I saw the appeal of him. He had a sweet face but he was definitely too much for Kallie.

"He ate them all when I was at work the other day."

"Cheese slice?" Kallie nodded at me and went back into the fridge then delivered it right to my hands, to avoid any quick movement that might startle him. I unwrapped the cheese as he continued to turn his head to each side. "You know where your bed is, big guy? The couch?"

I assumed before Kallie said a word, Bruce ran and jumped on the couch, the entire front lifts off before he settled down and the couch resets on the floor, not as loudly as I thought but still worrisome for the people who live directly below Kallie. I threw the cheese at the dog and immediately walked over to the kitchen, near Kallie to avoid Bruce's stare.

"So what now?" Kallie asked, just turning her head to look at me. I watched as her chest heaved up and down, it took me a moment to focus back on what she said. I cleared my throat to remind myself I was here as her friend not the kind of guy she'd fuck.

"Cleaning this mess up, obviously. Broom and dustpan are still in the pantry, right?" I stared as her lips opened, a question in her brows.

"Right, of course, because my brother lived here." She said out loud, after working out the question in her head.

I smirked, "Should I expect things to be moved around since a woman lives here now?"

Kallie hit my arm before my question rang back at me, "Hey, that's sexist."

"That hurt!" I feigned a sad face as I rubbed my arm. "That's not what I meant, though!"

"Yeah, I'm sure." She said as I walked to the pantry and pulled out the dustpan and broom.

"Hey, I am trying to be a gentleman."

Kallie chuckled as she tried to pull the dustpan and broom from my hands, "You? A gentleman? Hard to believe."

"I could take care of this for you." I state with my hands firmly around the handles, it'd been a while since we've stood this close to each other, and it felt good, whether or not it's from yearning the woman that's turned me down, or maybe it's just the feeling of something between us. Could she feel it, too?

"Yeah? There's nothing else you'd rather be doing?" Kallie asked playfully, I knew she didn't mean it in a flirtatious way, but I can't help but lean in a little more, I swore she did too as I feel her breath against my chin.

I almost got my lips on her before I heard the growling Dobermann behind us. I looked at the dog just to see his glare toward me with his teeth bared, the sound that came from his throat made me take a step back. And that's when I look at Kallie and watched her scramble as she pulled her hair back.

"Right, you meant Bruce's mess." She let go of the broom and dustpan and waved a hand for me to clean it for her. If it had been my way, I would've said yes to the mess while I took care of her, but the damn dog is another version of Lane. Even his eyes reminded me of Lane's.

Once I had cleaned up Kallie's living room, she ordered a pizza as a payment for the work I did for her. We ate and talked about parts of our lives that I had only shared with Lane. Kallie hadn't been anything like her brother, even if they weren't blood-related, they had a lot of physical similarities, but personality wise, they were opposites. It was hard to see how they connected and considered each other siblings. Even if it had been one foster house after another for them, their history was the only thing that kept them together as a family.

"The bed." Kallie said mid-bite, like I was supposed to know what she was referring to. My mind immediately went to assuming she wanted me sexually, but that couldn't be right.

"What?" I asked for clarification. She chuckled, and I swore a rare dimple appeared on her cheek, it might've been my favorite thing.

"Before," Kallie said, she covered her mouth as she chewed. I wanted to remove her hand so I could look at that dimple longer. "When you asked if I moved anything around. I moved the bed. Well, actually, I had his mattress thrown out and ordered my own because there was no way I was sleeping on his sex filled-mattress."

The laugh that tumbled out of me seemed to surprise her.

"What did I say?" She asked as she pulled her hair behind her ear.

"Sex filled-mattress. What the hell is that?" I asked, still laughing.

"What? You're saying if I didn't take a blacklight to it that it wouldn't have a bunch of gross sex stuff stuck to it?"

I laughed even harder, nearly falling on the floor. "Oh my god, that's an amazing visual."

"Shut up!" Kallie chuckled, "It's totally true, I know you're laughing because your bed is probably the same."

It took a couple deep breaths and coughs for me to regain myself, "Maybe. But I don't see how that's ever been a problem for any guy before. I guess I can see why a sister wouldn't want to, but that's what mattress covers and sheets are for."

"Well, I'm sorry, I was just excited to get my own bed and my own room."

"Fair." I nodded before I grabbed another slice of pizza. "Foster homes really made you appreciate living on your own, huh?"

"Ha. Yeah." She quieted up and that's when I realize there was more to be told. I let some silence pass by before I thought of the next thing to ask her, especially if I wanted her to talk more about her issues.

"There was more than just the foster-home?"

Her green eyes stared back at me with tears. My brows furrowed with confusion.

"Kallie?"

"I have to go." Her voice cracked as she got off the floor and ran to the bathroom, nearly slamming the door behind her. I didn't know what just happened, and I hesitated before I stood and walked to the bathroom door to get her to come out.

"Did I say something wrong, Kal? You can tell me. I'm pretty good at listening, remember?" I smirked, trying to lighten the mood. I could hear her sniffling on the other side of the door.

"Just go home, Jake. I'll be fine." Her voice didn't sound fine. I felt responsible for causing whatever just happened to her. Perhaps it was my new leaf, or just Kallie, but I wasn't going anywhere. What's worse was I couldn't remember the last time I cared about a crying woman, so I felt that I had to stay for a whole other reason. Whether she thought I left or not, I waited until the bathroom door opened and pulled her into me. I pulled her into my arms, for a hug. Another milestone that I never did with women.

"Jake, what are you doing?" She asked into my shoulder.

"Making you feel better. I hope." I answered, before I let her pull herself away.

"I thought you left." Kallie's eyes filled with tears again, as I pulled her hair behind her ear.

I sucked in a breath, "*Friends* don't let friends cry alone." The half-sob half-laugh that came from Kallie's mouth told me I had nailed this friend thing.

MIKA C.C.

"I'm sorry I ran off like that. I have a lot of – triggers and trauma. Not exactly something I like to focus on. It's hard for me to get out of my head once a memory pops in." Kallie said with a sad smile.

"I think I have *something* that can fix that."

"Are you telling me to hold on like a spider monkey?" Kallie's voice, as innocent as she sounded, also reminded me of the kind of girl that was up for a challenge.

"If you get on, you're gonna need to hold on like it's the first time you grabbed the chains to keep you from falling off a swing. Stay focused & balance. Hold your head high." I pulled up on my extra helmet, "If you get scared, you take a deep breath, but don't you dare let go. I've got you covered, I'm the chains that keep you from falling, got it?"

She nodded, even with my hand holding the helmet, I felt the slight pressure of her nod.

"When we're on the bike, our lives are the only thing that matters. I want you to understand when you put your life in my hands, I'm going to do whatever it takes to make sure you get to keep it."

What I didn't tell her, is the fact that I haven't driven any women on my bike before wasn't because I would be liable if anything happened, it was because no woman was worth the risk. Not one hookup, not one fling – none of them made me feel like – well none of them made me feel, period.

"Do you understand me, princess? I need you to use your words this time."

I felt her throat bob against my fingers before she answered me, "Yes, I understand. I promise to hold onto you and if I get scared... I'll just breathe and let you know."

"Good, I can always pull off to the side of the road if you need to get air outside of the helmet."

Though I couldn't see her eyes between the helmets, it felt like the rest of me knew she understood the words spoken and unspoken. The first ride was always the hardest, but I hoped—*God*, I hoped she would come to love it the way I did.

"You can let go of me now." Her voice shifted with the words, "I know what to do." Though she didn't see my smirk, I sure as hell hoped she'd feel better knowing I'd be keeping her safe the entirety of our ride.

I wanted to keep her first ride on my motorcycle short, but halfway through, I heard her voice through my helmet. She yelled, words that meant she enjoyed it. I thought for sure she'd be screaming to get off, but when I opened my visor to hear her. I heard her 'woohooing' more than a person would on a rollercoaster. With the dark sky and lights of the cars and buildings that zipped by us in a blink of an eye, I could only imagine the adrenaline it gave her. Every time I got on my bike it felt the same. By the time we made it back to her apartment, the tears were gone, replaced by a smile in her eyes and helmet hair. I chuckled as I took off my helmet.

"Liked it, huh?"

"It was definitely what I needed." Kallie's lips closed in a small smile. "Thank you, Jake."

"Anytime."

She chuckled, "I'm sure that'll be a one time thing, thanks though."

I followed her up to her apartment door as she turned and looked at me.

Her hair bounced as she asked, "You're coming back in?" I watched as her eyes danced to my lips before they locked with mine. I let my hand wrap around the back of her neck and pulled her to me, bending to place my lips on hers. Felt the pucker of her lips on mine, her hands were on my chest, her body trembled under my fingertips before I let her pull away.

"Right–" Kallie said, patting my chest, "That was nice. Goodnight." She opened the door and closed it right in my face before I had the chance to say goodnight back.

I felt my jaw clench as I stared at her apartment door, I wasn't going to knock or wait, she'd made it clear. Friends were all she wanted from me.

Chapter 7

Kallie

It had been a week since I had spoken a word to Jake, which made me feel bad because we'd agreed to be friends, but a lot happened the last time we hung out. It'd been our first time hanging outside of work and during that time, I almost had a full on breakdown, let Jake take me on my first motorcycle ride, and kissed him. Well, he kissed me, but I definitely didn't stop it, and I liked it. I really liked it. I thought the guy behind the motorcycle might've done it for me, but once Jake's lips met mine, I realized it was him, too. I was attracted to the office playboy and first guy friend I'd ever have. It was a bad idea to get mixed up with Jake, especially with him being best friend's with my brother.

There were plenty of reasons to end the friendship I had with Jake, ones that had nothing to do with a world-shattering kiss. The kiss had to mean nothing if I were going to stay friends with him and I couldn't justify that it meant nothing. I had felt something, something in my chest and lower, in between my legs being one of them. How could I tell Jake that our friendship had to come to an end?

I expected Nova to have some sort of advice when I went over to the new house to congratulate her and my brother. I had made cookies, and by made, I mean I bought the cookie packet that came from Publix that you just peeled a part from the packaging and put directly on a baking sheet and into the oven for ten minutes. When Nova answered the door I heard the screaming baby, she quickly took the tub of cookies from my arms and replaced them with the baby. Quinn's scream settled into nothing as she stared up at me. I held Quinn and walked into Nova's house with a fake smile.

"You know I love holding Quinn, but um–" I looked around for Nova to see her nowhere in the front room or living room. "Nova?"

"Sorry I had to run to the bathroom!" She yelled from somewhere. Quinn cooed as she grabbed my hair and tried to put it in her mouth.

"Is mommy going crazy?" I asked the baby, Quinn looked so much like Lane, with his eyes and the nose was uncanny, though she had her mom's sharp chin. When Nova re-appeared she looked less frantic than I recalled the way she looked when she opened the door. The unbrushed hair and pajamas had been replaced with a bun and a sundress.

"Thanks for the cookies." Nova said in a greeting tone before taking Quinn from my arms.

"And fixing your daughter." I added it for her.

"That too." Nova chuckled, "Babies are hard."

I looked her up and down, seeing her growing belly as she held Quinn. "Do you want me to hold her again?"

"Would you?" The way Nova's voice broke, told me she needed a break. She didn't need to hear my drama, but I had already stepped into her domain so I had to let her talk it out, she probably needed it more.

"How are you doing?" I asked as we sat on the couch, I lightly bounced Quinn on my knee, "And I mean, you, not the baby or Lane or the baby growing inside you."

"Don't let me get pregnant again." Nova said with a hand on my free leg. "I'm exhausted all the time, and I've been nonstop sick for months and I think I have zero bladder control."

I didn't mean to laugh but I felt it slip out, "If you ever need me to take the baby for the day." I offered as my nights of texting Jake were about to be freed up.

"I would totally say yes, but not with Bruno."

"You mean Bruce?"

"Oh, right. That's another thing to add to the list, 'mom brain'. Yesterday I thought I forgot to eat, so last night I went downstairs to grab something light. Well Lane woke me up this morning holding the baby and wondering why all the baby food was in bed with me. I had eaten three jars of Quinn's food." Nova let out a little laugh, "I need coffee."

"I think you need sleep." I retorted back.

"That's it!" She said, standing.

"You're going to take a nap while I take care of Quinn and clean up your living room?"

"What?" Nova looked at the floor full of baby toys, "Absolutely not. That's Lane's job." She paused for emphasis, "Let's go get some coffee and baby food for Quinny here." Nova bended and grabbed the baby from my lap and held her up high as Quinn laughed.

"So this is the unofficial official coffee shop for you baseball nerds, huh?" I asked as I take in the space as Nova found a table that fits Quinn's stroller and us.

"Okay, we're not going to be mean here, because the owner has done a lot for me. Not to mention she's scary." Nova said as we both grab our coffees from the pickup line and sit at a table.

"I'm just curious, what's so special about this space?" I looked around again, the Tampa and St Pete skylines were wallpapered on opposite walls of each other, the wooden eclectic theme made the space feel inviting and warm, but I didn't get why our baseball team frequented here the most.

"Nova!"

"Madison!" Nova yelled back, and stood up from her seat, she scooted her belly out of her spot to hug the woman that recognized her. As I sat there feeling awkward and slightly left out.

"You must be Kallie." Madison said as she looks down at me. I immediately felt my mood lift, as I stood up to introduce myself.

"Yeah, that's me, how'd you know that?" I asked, greeting her with a handshake, Madison's hand took mine and we shook for a moment before her hand pulled back. She looked a little uncomfortable from our touch and I didn't know if I should be offended.

"Lane." Madison rolled her eyes, "He's a big yapper, way more than my friends. Which is honestly saying something because we've stayed out countless nights at the bar."

"Do you still go to Pete's?"

I watched as Madison smacked her leg, "Not really. I wish! Everyone out here is having babies." She said as she looked down at Nova's growing belly.

Nova nervously laughed, "Ha, I can't keep it in my pants."

Madison looked over at me, "What about you? Are you pregnant, too?"

I opened my mouth to answer her as Nova whispered in Madison's ear. I noticed as Madison's eyes grew wide.

"What!?" Madison's mouth dropped open.

"Nova!" I yelled.

"What? It's Madison, who's she gonna tell?" Nova shrugged.

"Besides Christian?" Madison held her hands together.

"Hayes?!" I yelled again, with my eyes widened.

Madison nervously laughed, "Wow, so this is what power feels like."

After Nova sweetly outed my secret to her coffee-bestie, I had to explain almost everything to the two of them. It took Nova going to the bathroom for me to finally take a break from explaining my virginity. Even Madison took a moment from our conversation to help customers before she slid back into her chair, she looked at me with a gleam in her eyes.

"What?" I asked with furrowed brows.

"You're leaving out something."

I took a sip of my coffee, "Nope. You two now know more than anyone else. Which means vault of secrets."

"Circle of trust sounds better." Madison retorted, "I wasn't referring to your virginity. I was referring to you having another secret."

My brows raised as I smiled, "Yeah? Well I just met you, I don't think I should be spilling all my secrets." I looked down at my coffee cup.

"Is it a crush?"

"Not a crush." I shook my head as I stared at the creamer separating from my coffee.

"Hm. So if it's not a crush, it's a guy." Madison said, pushing.

I looked at her for a moment, "Right, because that's so hard to guess from looking at me."

"Ooo, sarcasm, my first language." Madison rubbed her hands together, "Must be someone you work with."

My eyes widened before I looked away from her.

"Wow, I got that right!" She sounded proud of herself, "I've been studying body language for all of thirty days and I can't believe I figured that out. So the guy has to be someone who works in baseball, now if I deduct the married guys from the players..."

I rolled my eyes as she did math with her fingers.

"It's Jake!" Both of us answered in unison. Madison's mouth dropped open.

"Wait, really?"

"You were going to get there eventually."

"I'm just –" Madison's expression froze, "Jake, really?"

"We've just been trying to be friends and the other night he really comforted me, and then he sort of– *kissed* me."

Madison's expression didn't change, if anything she looked more like a robot. I could only imagine she'd thought it over in her head. Maybe she hadn't a thought at all, she could've be trying to find the words to say to run away from the conversation.

"It's nothing. I mean, I obviously have to end our friendship but it's for the best." I said to fill the quiet between us, but Madison's face shifted.

"What? Why?"

"Because... Can people of the opposite gender even still be friends after a kiss?" I seriously asked her.

"I mean, *yeah*? Beckett and I are still friends and we've had sex."

I shook my head wrapping my head around the words, "Wait, you had sex with an umpire?"

"Yeah. Also, sex doesn't need to be whispered, we're grown ups here."

"I just need you to back up and tell me this story." With the hope that Nova didn't hear me asking Madison for advice.

"Definitely not going to do that, I can't summarize real life events. Plus it doesn't matter, if you still want to be friends with Jake, you can just *pretend* it didn't happen." She shrugged, "I kissed my best friend's husband the night we first met, and that's never been an issue."

"Oh, so you're like full-on weird." I retorted back.

"Ha. Funny." Madison paused, "Just tell him you want nothing else to happen between you two."

"I'm sure that's easier said than done, but what I have planned is–"

"*Or,*" Madison began, "Instead of your plan, you can make him fall in love with you so that way you're not the only one in love with him."

"I love how close you think we are." I said to her, "I don't *love* Jake, I don't even like him ninety-percent of the time. It finally felt like we were getting to be good friends and then one kiss blew it up."

She shrugged and looked away, "You can't turn off feelings for a person, just so you know. I tried, it doesn't work."

I almost asked her what she meant but as soon as I follow Madison's gaze, Nova returned back to the table with Quinn in her arms and I'm left to stew on whatever it was that Madison meant...

Chapter 8

Jake

I've always done a good job at taking one for the team, I've even taken initiative when needed, but the last few days I've been off my game. I haven't been able to hit a ball, haven't been able to catch one either. Coach Guntz said I was going through the yips but there was no way. If I was going through the yips there would've been more signs than missing a ball or two. Even when I hit the showers, I felt off.

Kallie had really gotten under my skin and now here I was worried that I did something wrong. Maybe I had. Maybe I took the wrong initiative with her, but she didn't exactly pull back right away. Even when I tried to get her off my mind during practice games my mind would wander, and then my eyes would deceive me and look at the window of Nova's office. I swore I saw Kallie staring me down, watching me play my worst. God, if that had been the case, throw me off a bridge. I never liked anyone seeing me play a rough game. Even with the last two games we played, it wasn't nearly as bad as Coach made it seem. At least that's what Hayes and Lane had told me.

Even with it all on the field it felt like I was holding back, I couldn't tell if it was a mental thing or something physical. Had I played my last game? Had my best been behind me already? Was I out of shape? Was I not eating my best? Or was it the fact that I hadn't had sex? Was it the gut-wrenching denial from Kallie as she slammed her door in my face? None of them I could answer on my own. So I started from the bottom and worked my way up. I wasn't going to have sex, but I did have a hand that could do the job for me, I did have a sex toy that reminded me of a good time.

Last on my list was making amends with Kallie whether she liked it or not. I had to try something, anything. And I thought of a good one. The idea of it came to me a while ago but now it was more feasible, especially with me trying to get back in her good graces. She hadn't texted or called me back in over two weeks and I was dying. Never did I think I'd put a friendship on a pedestal, yet alone give a friend a gift, especially not a small, furry friend.

Again, the idea behind it was there, Cherry was a rescue and some type of mutt but looked closest to a basset hound. When I got her from the pound, they had told me she was super friendly, low maintenance *and* didn't chew or destroy any kind of pillows or decorative blankets. The biggest selling point was that the dog wasn't Bruce, getting Bruce out wasn't an issue either though. There was a teammate looking for a dog he could train, he wanted a big dog, wanted one that was big and intimidating like him. And I had set up the trade with him, only if Kallie agreed to it...

It took me knocking on her door three times before Kallie finally answered the door. I had to hide Cherry in a box with holes, and even though I wanted Kallie to see my face first, I realized the box with a bow on it might've been a better selling point. So when she answered the door I didn't get to see the look on her face, I didn't hear the sounds of excitement of a present, just a long silence. By the time I looked over the box, I could see the look of confusion on her face. I might've even seen a little bit of hurt written on Kallie's features.

"Listen, Jake. I think we should talk."

"And I think before you talk you should let me talk first." I said with an awkward smile as I held the box as still as I could without dropping the dog inside.

"Come in." I followed her slowly to the kitchen and set down the box with my arm on the lid, hoping Cherry wouldn't blow my cover completely.

I didn't realize Kallie's given me the floor to speak first until her eyes and brows heightened for a moment.

"Oh, right." I started to compose myself and tried hard to remember the lines I prepared to memorize. "Kallie, I realize the kiss might've been stupid and selfish, and maybe I was, but that's on me not you. I fully own up to my mistake. I still want to be your friend and want to be a part of your life. I'm sorry if that kiss made any indication that I wanted something else."

There's a quick beat of silence before I continue.

"You may be thinking what's in the box, and I'm gonna tell you. But I do want to say, it wasn't my intention to fuck things up so bad that we couldn't even talk to each other. I like getting to see you, talking to you and I want good things for you. So this present is more of a *you deserve better,* kind of thing."

Kallie stepped forward, meeting me close to the counter, "I accept your apology. And your present, if it's good." She smiled lightly at me before she put her hands on the lid. I lifted my arm off the lid as she opened it, and the box moved.

Kallie's eyes grew wide as she looked down then up at me, "Really, Jake? Another dog?"

"You get to keep this one, and I take the other one." I said with a smile, "That's the real present."

"What? You're taking Bruce?"

"Not me, personally." I answered her with a hand to my chest, "There's actually someone on the team that wants a dog just like him, so I told him about Bruce and he's willing to take care of him."

Kallie's brows furrowed as she pulls Cherry out of the box and cuddled her, I swore I saw tears line her eyes. "That's the sweetest thing anyone has ever done for me, Jake." She didn't look right at me as she nuzzled her head against the dog's neck but Cherry immediately started licking Kallie. She laughed as the dog continued to lick her until she petted Cherry and set her down.

I decided to give Kallie the low-down of all of Cherry's personality and age, "She's potty-trained, she doesn't speak a lot. She comes with a lot of toys and as you can tell is super friendly. Oh and her name is Cherry."

"Cherry?" Kallie asked, she looked up at me as she petted her new dog.

"Like Cherry Coke." Both of us said, in unison.

I gave her a wink, "Your favorite drink."

Kallie stood up and pulled me in for a hug. I hesitated, knowing something this intimate could lead to another mistake. I let my arms briefly hold her back, just long enough until she pulled away. I couldn't help but look at the tears that rimmed Kallie's sapphire eyes. There's a part of me that wanted to wipe away her tears, but even that I held back from. I was not her boyfriend, I was not even sure if we're still friends.

"Thank you Jake." She almost said with a sob, "But how are we gonna keep this angel from meeting the demon?"

"I got that covered too." I smiled at her and I swear the little smile she gave me back is more than just hope, it's friendship renewed.

After three days of being back in Kallie's good graces, and one day of moving Bruce and his entire existence out of Kallie's apartment, I received the text I'd been waiting for. It's not exactly something to be excited about, but having a friendship with Kallie made me crave things I didn't know were possible. The things I craved were as simple as her attention, being around her, her telling me about some stupid date and going on long walks with her and Cherry.

Maybe I had started to become a version of whipped I'd never seen before, especially as a guy who didn't have a girlfriend and wasn't having sex with anyone but himself. It was a mood, a view, and a pleasure I think was made just for me. Or maybe it was just a phase.

Whatever it was, I wasn't letting go of the feeling of being better—for me.

The text I had been waiting for was silly to some, but it meant I got the go ahead to come over, Kallie was trusting me again, and I wasn't going to feel bad for what had happened. It was going to be like nothing ever happened.

"So I need you to sit on this side of the couch while I sit over here." Kallie said, as she placed four large throw pillows in between us.

"This is not what I had in mind when you said we could still be friends."

"It's just to keep a normal, safe distance, maybe because I still haven't gotten to tell you my side."

"Your side?" I asked with a curved brow.

"Yeah, you know how you wanted to go first because you had the dog? I had stuff I wanted to say beforehand, remember?"

"Oh right. Duh. Well, why haven't you told me yet?"

Kallie looked at me for a long moment, "That's why I invited you over, or is that not implied?"

"Gotcha." I nodded, I could see the wheels turning in her mind. Like she definitely still saw me as the dumb blonde of the team. Her face contorted as I noticed Kallie looked a little more uncomfortable at whatever she was going to say.

"As my friend, I think it's time you know something about me. Something I keep a big secret. Like it's probably bigger than my abandonment issues."

"Bigger than Space Jam 2 being horrible?"

"Exactly." She pointed at me, as if she understood a thing I said. I guaranteed she hadn't watched the movie, but watching her squirm as she tried to piece together what she just agreed to was fun.

"I'm all ears then, Princess." I said with a smile. Kallie looked at me with an evil eye as she shook her head and tried not to smile back. At least I could cheer her up even with whatever's heavy that held her mind.

"I'm a virgin."

I settled deeper into the couch as I let the words process, "Can you say that one more time?"

"Jake. I am a virgin. A twenty-five year old virgin. And I don't mean just sex. I mean like the most I've ever done is kiss a guy. And before you and I kissed, well I hadn't kissed a guy in – like ten months?"

I didn't know what was more important in Kallie's explanation, the fact that she's entrusting me with her secret, or that the secret is something to be protected. Part of me believes the reason she told me was because of the kiss, but I didn't think it would be such a pivotal moment for her.

"I'm not expecting you to say anything, just thought you should know as my friend. I do ask that you keep my secret and not tell my brother."

There was more, there had to have been, especially with the way she looked away from me. Whether or not she wanted to speak of it was on her. I didn't want to say anything to trigger her, I didn't want to ask if it'd bring back bad memories for her.

"So, you're a virgin. I'm a manwhore, it's like we cancel each other out." I said with a smile, with hope that would changed her mood. Kallie looked back at me and I saw the playful glint in her eyes.

"I guess we do." Kallie agreed, seeming more comfortable now that she'd gotten her secret off her chest. "I wonder if we cancel each other out on other things?"

"We'd have to talk *all* night then." I answered with a brow raised.

Chapter 9

Kallie

I never thought having a guy know about my virginity would be so therapeutic, but after telling Jake it seemed like a weight off my chest. My friendship seemed stronger and Jake seemed to not only take it well, but he might've even acted sensitive toward my virginity. I was so expecting Jake to ask me if it was my choice, if it was brought on by anything or if he could fix it. Maybe I had expected it so much that it was weird that he didn't because part of me did want him to push me for more.

The kiss was now known as The Incident and we'd reached twenty-four days since The Incident. We even managed not to bring it up in any conversations. The more we hung out the more The Incident was replaced with The Time Jake Bought Me A Dog. There didn't seem to be any bad feelings toward Jake, and it felt like he reciprocated.

MIKA C.C.

After living in Florida for so long I had thought for sure I'd see Jake in a regular shirt, but it seemed nearly impossible. He had this affinity for long sleeves, it might've been because he rode a motorcycle, but it also looked like he was hot all the time. It wasn't like I wanted to see him shirtless, I just expected the guy would be more comfortable in a regular t-shirt. Jake even wore long sleeves on the baseball field. It made me think that maybe he also didn't like showing his skin off, possibly the same way I didn't. I didn't like showing a lot of my skin, I had the complexion of my native ancestors, so I wanted to keep it protected. But what I didn't get was Jake's reasoning.

"So there's a lot of speculation." I started, hoping to get a reaction out of Jake, but his face stayed straight as he looked at me through the camera. We were on a facetime call after he'd just finished an away game. The idea of video-chatting was his idea, and I didn't say no.

"What about?"

"That you're really hairy." I answered, with my hand almost over my mouth, I couldn't stand looking at myself on the facetime call, so I tried to just focus on Jake's face.

He chuckled as his perfect teeth showed, his blonde hair bounced as he moved his camera closer toward his face, I could almost see up his nostrils.

"I think this is the only place I'm the hairiest. I try to keep my hair one, short length, all over."

"Attractive." My sarcasm spoke.

"Oh, you're talking about my body aren't you?"

"Kind of. I've only seen you with long-sleeves so I can't deny these rumors that you're just really hairy under your uniform." I answered, hoping to get him to bite.

Jake pulled his phone back, "Princess, are you trying to undress me with your words?" He teased.

"What? No! I was simply just curious as to why you only wear long sleeves and jeans in the Florida weather."

"For one, they're sun protection sleeves, so they don't make me feel hot. They're actually very cooling for me and keep my skin protected. Two, jeans are just a fashion choice. Trust me, cargo shorts are not attractive and basketball shorts are just glorified versions of them. I'd wear Chubbies but they're not really socially acceptable." Jake explained with a glare in his eyes.

"Okay that makes sense. I was just wondering because – rumors." I sighed and shrugged my shoulders slightly. I didn't know what to expect but I hadn't thought he'd have a reasonable explanation for his clothing. I may have sounded just a little disappointed that he had no follow up questions.

"I should probably shower. The guys want to go out drinking and I agreed to one and only one drink." Jake stated as he put his phone down somewhere in the bathroom, I only know because of the shower in the background.

I nodded and looked at him as he ran a hand through his hair. "Okay I'll let you –" One moment Jake had his shirt on and the next it's off him completely. I was left to just ogle him through a phone, unable to zoom in on every tattoo that covered every space of his arms, his very muscled and toned arms. He'd got a big tattoo across his chest and his stomach had no tattoos though he did have a mini-strip of hair near his belly button.

"There's your proof." Jake said, as he his pecs dance. His words reminded me of the reason why he stripped his shirt off in the first place.

"I will make sure every girl knows. Not hairy. Just heavily – tattooed." I stated with a loose breath.

Jake picked up his phone and I swore I saw the muscled veins that go from his hand to forearm for the first time, "Is there something making you—feel different?"

I sucked in a sharp breath, and tried not to give notice to the warmth between my legs. I knew I was attracted to Jake, but this felt like more. There's a need for something I couldn't reach, I couldn't explain the feeling.

I pulled back my bangs behind my ear, "No, of course not. Just wasn't expecting all the tattoos."

"They need protection from the sun, so wearing the sleeves makes sure the color doesn't fade or blur out."

"That makes – understandable. Though I wouldn't know because I've never considered a tattoo before." I felt myself yapping longer than necessary. "I should let you get your shower."

Jake bit his bottom lip, "Sorry if I caused any problems. I'll see you tomorrow morning though, yeah?"

"Definitely." I threw a finger-gun at him and hung up my phone before I did something more embarrassing.

I tossed in bed for hours wondering how I did this to myself. I was in a predicament where my body was begging to be touched, and I didn't know the first thing about touching myself. I didn't know where my fingers went, did they work the outside or inside? Was I to move my fingers up and down or roll them in a circle? I couldn't even gain the confidence to google how to take care of myself, even after I tried touching my opening for three minutes, then playing with an area that didn't seem to do anything. It took me putting an extra pillow between my legs to feel something and even then didn't make me feel any better. The aggravation of it all caused me to give up, so I focused on trying to sleep again...

I woke up to a knocking on my door, Cherry lightly barked as I barely got my robe on me when I swung the door open to Jake standing with a box of donuts. I tried not to smile but it's hard when I spent most of my night thinking of a shirtless him, add in the food and it was just a bonus. I didn't hug him to avoid any of my feelings from resurfacing the night before. The last thing I needed was any more feelings for my friend.

"I thought of early morning donuts and then taking Cherry for a walk?" Jake asked as his way of greeting me. I opened the door wider for him to come in. He placed the box on the counter and looked at me up and down. "Didn't realize I woke you."

"It's fine." I said trying to close my robe more than it is, the full length does a good job of hiding my skin from the kind of guy I would've once considered him, but now I considered his gaze a compliment.

"Want me to put your coffee on?" Jake asked me as he grabbed a donut and took a bite. I couldn't help but want to be the donut as I watched his lips.

"I want you to kiss me again." He stared at me with ruffled brows.

"What? No, I'm not doing that again. I don't want to lose you as a friend."

"I think I need it though." I nearly whined the words.

Jake scoffed, "You don't, you just think you do."

"I have this need, Jake and I can't fix it."

He chuckled and put the donut down, "Get a toy, use your fingers, that's how women deal with it." He tries to walk to the living room but I stop him.

"I don't know how." I said with my hands turned into fists, "I'm running on two hours of sleep because I couldn't figure out which finger goes where. By the time I googled it was showing me from a guys perspective not a female."

"You seriously googled how to finger yourself?"

"I am new to this, it's not exactly something you're taught in school. So yeah, I googled it. And now I'm asking you, and I don't know if you want to call it a favor or what, but I trust you. I know you know what you're doing because every woman that's talked about you has never said a bad thing about the sex."

Jake smirked before his smile fell, "Still, there's about a million reasons why this shouldn't happen and even if I wanted it to-"

"So you do want to?"

He rolled his eyes with his jaw clenched, "I'm trying to prove I can be a good guy, not the asshole manwhore that takes his best friend's sister's virginity."

"Who says you have to take my virginity? I'm not asking you to have sex with me, I'm asking for your help with everything else."

Jake's green eyes stared back at me, "Everything else?"

"Teach me, Jake. Please." I tried to kiss him but I could only reach part of his bottom lip from my height. I decided to undo the tie on my robe and opened it so he can see me in my short pajama bottoms and the tank top I wore to bed.

I watched as his eyes roamed over me, "Please, Jake. Please?" He exhaled as he put his hands on my hips, his palms warmed me and his fingertips made my skin tingle, as I took a deep breath and looked up at him. Imagining him saying something like, *you're telling me you want me to touch you, taste you and feel you, and I don't even get to brag about it?*

"Fuck it." Jake whispered before he bent until our lips met in a quick movement. I felt his hands wrap around me further the longer our lips stayed connected. One of his hands traveled until it pulled the back of my neck, changing the position of my head—deepening our kiss, with his tongue pushed into my mouth until both of our tongues mingled.

We made out for a while until his hand came back down to my waist and he pulled me up on the counter. My ass hardly reacted to the cold granite countertops, until his lips pull from mine and I felt the warmth of him leave me.

"I'm going to need a minute to process this." He stated, followed by an exhale.

"Okay, I mean if it helps I think we should keep our friendship status."

"Good. Good. Just friends, friends with benefits." Jake agreed with a nod, with his hands on his hips.

"Is everything okay?" I asked as he looked like he's about to burst.

"If I keep touching you, I won't stop. It's been months without real sex for me. I know it's been way longer for you, but guys are – let's just say, our situations are different."

"Right." I chuckled, reminding myself of the video I found of a guy pleasing himself on google. It wasn't exactly an attractive video, but I did get to see how guys handled themselves.

"Do we need rules? Like a safe word?"

"What's a safe word?"

"It's when you need me to stop or slow down. Mostly stop though." He said, still sounding frantic.

"What about donut holes?" I asked with a look at the box of donuts. Jake's blank stare tells me my suggestion is vetoed. I jumped off the counter and walked towards him, I grabbed his hands and looked up at him as his eyes met mine. "I think we can figure it out as we move forward."

"If you ever feel uncomfortable I need you to tell me. I don't want you running off, crying or not. You give the word that we're done with this and I'll go right back to being your friend. We can pretend that nothing happened like before." Jake explained, looking me in the eye. I let his hands go and let him grab my face, "Remember what I said before your first ride?"

I nodded in answer and smiled, "Yeah."

"The same applies here, princess."

I pulled at his forearms on me and let him lean in as our lips crashed together. He pulled me back up on the counter thus starting a make-out session that I had no idea would get me there. Not with the more he kissed me the more his tongue danced in my mouth—the more his hands roamed my back, stomach, and thighs. Jake's fingers were ever careful not to touch a space I might've disapprove of, until I grabbed his hand and put it in between my legs. I moaned, hardly able to hear anything else with his fingers touching me. Even with his touch over my clothes, my tongue dances more with his, until I felt a warm release between my thighs. Jake barely touched me and yet I felt the release of whatever he did.

Our lips disconnect and I look at the look of satisfaction on his face, the grin, his darkened green eyes and the way his breath matches mine. I smiled back at him, finally feeling the contentment I'd been searching for since last night. Jake took a step back and sighed, excusing himself to the bathroom, and that's when I wondered if I did or didn't do something I should have.

Chapter 10

Jake

I thought kissing and touching Kallie after so long of waiting mixed with lust would be a solution to everything my brain told me was wrong. Instead it was almost the opposite. It was the problem, my brain screamed that what I was doing with Kallie was right, and yet a separate part of me told me it was wrong. It didn't help that making her come from rubbing my fingers against her cotton shorts was going to undo me right there in her kitchen. The sound of Kallie's moan, the feel of her wetness through her shorts were all that I needed to come, too. I ran off to her bathroom before I had the chance to explain the mess I made of my own underwear. I had to throw them out in her trash and hoped to God she wouldn't look or question why.

I'd never been embarrassed before, I hadn't came in my pants like that since I was teen, and the idea of explaining the whole thing to Kallie nearly killed me. I would've died right in her bathroom if it didn't hit me in the head that Kallie didn't know, as the innocent virgin who couldn't even get herself off. I was able to just tell her that I had to relieve myself after getting her off and she understood. Was it really a lie when I got off to her either way?

Agreeing to be Kallie's teacher of sorts was not in my plan. I was supposed to get to know her first, I was supposed to let her see me and now I was wooing her until I came in my own pants. I'd never let myself live it down. I was letting something else happen between us, knowing I could get burned, if not by her, then possibly by Lane. There was so much to lose, but the sound of her pleading ringing in my ears just told me it needed to be me. If not me, she'd find someone else and I couldn't let that happen.

I imagined the next three days would be Kallie constantly asking for my help but instead we were both so busy with work I hardly was able to come visit her office. I was told Kallie had some big project for the team coming up and that had been the first I heard her name in the last two days. I checked my phone to see if she texted me, hoping she'd let me know the project first, but there'd been nothing.

On my way out of practice with the rest of the team, I finally saw her in the parking garage. Her car was parked next to my bike, I didn't know if she'd parked there on purpose but I couldn't help but smile at her. But when Lane walked right in front of me before I had the chance to say hello to her, I decided to change my mood.

Lane talked to his sister for all of ten minutes before he moved out of the way to let me say hi. Instead, I decided to play a game with her.

"You wanna ride?"

She shakes her head, "No thanks. I don't like the idea of being the thousandth woman on your bike."

"What makes you think that?" I smirked.

"You mean besides you're a bit of a playboy? You look the type to do whatever it takes to get laid. I'm sure that line works with every cleat chaser."

"Maybe." The answer was yes, it did work on every girl. But the truth was that I never really meant it any other time. Sure I'd take girls for rides, but they always knew it would end sex. Something told me that Kallie needed it. Even with the game we played in front of her brother. The pink on her cheeks should've told me already, but I waited to hear the words from her lips.

"I've uh– I've never been on a motorcycle before." She said, lying in front of me and her brother, "you know because they're death traps."

I blew out a breath, thinking that maybe she may have meant it about the bike. I couldn't tell if she did it on purpose to piss me off or just to play along. Whether she believed it or not, voicing her feelings face to face was brave, not just something that someone has shoved up their asses.

Still I pushed, "so that's a no? Like a hard no, or maybe someday or just never?"

"Do you and my brother live in the same brain cell? You act so much like him."

I smiled at that, "are you trying to say being like your brother is a bad thing? I see it as a good thing."

Kallie rolled her eyes at me, as she looked between me and her brother. Another daring move for her. Lane shrugged.

"The first ride changes you." Was all Lane dared to say.

"That's it. Come on, get on the bike." I swatted at the seat in the back.

"What? I just told you no."

"No means no, I get that. But are you absolutely sure, when I have an extra helmet?"

Her dark brows raised slightly when I pulled out Lane's old helmet that he left at my house. Lane even looked tempted.

"Is that all the safety you have for me?"

"I have gloves and a helmet. That usually is it. Do you need the whole shebang? Not many people ride with full gear."

"I like to be thorough." She said with her lips turning up, "Plus I'm wearing jeans and a blouse. Not exactly riding material."

Lane interrupted, "I'll give you my jacket if you want to be his backpack for a little. I trust Jake on the bike, just make sure she gets to her car when you're done."

I nodded and tried to wink just at her, "See, even your brother approves of the ride."

Kallie looked between us again as she dropped her purse. "Fine. Let me just put my purse away." I waited until she locked her car and shoved the keys into her pocket. Lane threw his leather jacket at her and she put it on, it's about three sizes too big, but she shrugged and zipped it to make it look as if it belonged on her body. I preferred the pajamas to her covered up like this but for a ride I accepted it. Lane peaced out before I noticed Kallie as she started to put on the helmet. I helped her get it over her chin. I pulled up the visor to stare at her gorgeous blue eyes.

"Ready for a ride with yours truly, Princess?"

"Of course." I couldn't see her smile through the helmet just a little up tick of her cheeks and a quick wink.

I took her through the downtown road of St Pete before I got on the backroads and went fast. Kallie screamed like last time. This time I felt her adrenaline pump to her heart with how much more she held onto me, Kallie's chest had never been tighter against my back and I loved it, even with the whip of the air that passed by at every turn, I've never felt so comfortable as I do with her right where she was behind me. By the time I took Kallie back to her car in the garage, I could feel the mood shift. Kallie handed me back my extra helmet and I debated offering her to hold onto it. Being a backpack can be nerve-wracking but it could also be an honor to those who respect the bike. I watched as she turned to head towards her car, I didn't hate watching her leave but I knew the other way was ten times better.

"Goodnight, Princess." I said as I take off my helmet just for a brief moment, I could feel my hair stick to my forehead and the sweat on my neck. Kallie turned back to look at me, before I saw her walk in a fast-paced line right for my bike. I held onto my bike not knowing what to expect, especially when her hands wrapped around my face and she pulled my lips to hers. My gloved hand wrapped around her waist and I pulled her closer to me, letting her taste my tongue and my growing need for her. Kallie's lips parted with a sly smile on her face.

"See you tomorrow, Ghost Rider." Kallie's smile never splitting, she patted my chest, "You get that he's a character that rides a motorcycle, right?"

I chuckled, "Yeah, Princess, I get it. Now get home and get some sleep so I can wake you up in the morning." I answered with a wink. Kallie stepped out of me and walked back to her car, having given me another perfect view of her figure and her squeezable thighs.

There had been a brief moment of clarity when starting this friends with benefits thing with Kallie, that I just might find what I'm looking for within what we're doing. As quickly as that thought came, it passed when Lane's name flashed on my phone. I was halfway to Kallie's when I answered the call and let him talk into my ear for the next fifteen minutes. It turned out Lane needed a friend the same morning I was going to give Kallie her first lesson. I ended up calling her and let her know plans had changed due to her brother unknowingly cockblocking me.

One thing I promised myself was that if things got serious with Kallie I would tell Lane. In my head I had it all planned out, I wasn't planning on doing anything more with Kallie than she allowed, I was planning to tell her if I needed things to change between us. I wasn't actively dating, but I wasn't going to stop her from seeing other guys, so if I found someone who fit my lifestyle I'd let them. I couldn't see Kallie following my path completely; she had a family in Florida, had a niece, she even had another friend I didn't know about, she briefly mentioned that the friend was female but never gave me more than that.

I never thought of my family anymore, my mom left when I was ten, my dad died of brain cancer when I was thirteen, and I found out my mom followed his lead later that year. Whatever drugs they had done when they were young were the main reason why I didn't follow their footsteps, why I didn't work behind a desk with a standard nine to five. It was why I didn't put so much time and energy into becoming a doctor just for it to be taken away by a cancer diagnosis. For the rest of my formative years I was raised by my grandpa who was the sole reason why I wanted to be a major league baseball player. I had read every article of my grandpa making it to the minors, he almost made it to the majors if he didn't suffer a shoulder injury. It was right to follow his footsteps, to prove to him that not only his family could do it, but so he could live vicariously through me. Even knowing he was watching me in an assisted living home was good enough for me. The motorcycle helped me get over my fears of both life and death, so when Lane called me from a motorcycle dealership, I just knew it meant he needed me, and as quickly as possible.

"Remember when you used to have a motorcycle?" I snorted as I couldn't help but reminisce of the times where it was just me and Lane, fucking around on some bikes while fucking chicks left and right. We had good times together, before he went and fucked it up. I still loved the guy but man, if I took a picture of him now and went back in time to show his past self he'd say I was fucking with him. No way would he ever believe he'd be in love with someone, so deeply that he stayed when he knocked her up, and that now he was a dad, not just a dad of one kid, but also had another on the way. There's no way that *that* Lane Capsley would believe me.

"I do. Ah good times." Lane answered as he sighed and looked over to his wife, "We should get a family bike."

"What?" Nova's smile dropped, "There's no such thing as a family bike, Lane."

"Oh, Nova baby, there's always such a thing as a family bike." He said pointing to a bike at the dealership.

"Lane, you couldn't handle a bike now. Why are you guys even here?"

"I've been trying to figure that out myself." Nova replied before looking at her husband.

"I just think it's time for a change." Lane said with a stiff smile.

Not even two days later, I parked my bike just at the right time. My Princess walked by showing off her cute style. Kallie barely looked at me, but I knew she could feel me staring, even if it's with my helmet on, she even quickened her step as if she didn't think I could catch up to her. Just as I started to get off my bike, the revving of another motorcycle caused my head to turn, as I turned to see the bike park next to mine. I go to take off my helmet but the mystery biker took off their helmet first.

"Fuck, I forgot what it felt like to ride a bike." Lane exclaimed with a large smile, "It's like fucking my girl for the first time in our four week break."

"What the shit is this? Nova just let you get a fucking bike?"

Lane chuckled, "Who said I needed Nova's acceptance?"

My head dipped to the side, "Are you trying to get in deep shit with your *pregnant* wife?"

"There's no deep shit necessary. It's not like she can ride it. I can *and* I needed something to blow off steam from, well, getting blowjobs all the time."

"You do realize how dumb you sound right?" I paused with a hope he'd say something smart, when he doesn't I continue, "You know it's bad when I'm the one sounding like the voice of reason."

Lane laughed, "Yeah, but you only live once. I didn't say I was gonna keep it, just that I needed to blow off steam."

My brows furrowed, "What kind of steam do you need to blow off?"

I watched my friend's face drop, "Nothing, bro." He shook his head, "It's stupid stuff. No worries."

There's a big part of me that wants to say fuck it and make my best friend tell me but at the same time, I know it's not the right time. Lane has always been pretty good at telling me when something bugged him, he's always been vocal with Nova too, I've noticed. Whatever it is that goes past his face is not something he's ready for, and I don't think I can help him on that front. It actually reminded me a lot of the way I have had to wait for Kallie to tell me things on her terms.

"Ready for Guntz to rip us a new one?" I changed the subject as I shed my sweater off.

"It's my favorite time of the day, of course I'm ready." He answered with a wink. I offered my knuckles to him, which always started as a fist bump but turned into our secret handshake. Call it immature but we've been doing it since college and we'll probably never let it end.

By the time Lane and I made it to the field Coach Guntz had us running drills, whatever was shoved up his ass told me the dude was dealing with something personal. I couldn't stand it, not when I had missed another three days of seeing Kallie, when I had promised her I would help her learn how touching herself would be an experience for both of us. She was so excited and then the game and her work got in the way of it.

Just when I thought practice was over, Guntz pulled me into his office.

"You know that we're still doing the retreat for the players that need the most help, right?"

"Yeah, Lane told me it was set in motion months ago." I answered Guntz, knowing that Lane and Nova had set it up for the players that had trouble getting along. While most of the team had gotten better at communicating and working together, there were still a few of us that needed the extra push. Zach and Nick, my teammates, who were constantly at each other's throats were the ones to worry about the most.

"I added you to the roster."

My brows raised, "What? Coach, respectfully I don't need any team building exercises."

"No, but you've guaranteed our losses the last four games. We were World Series Champs last season, remember? I'm not having one of my star players make a mockery of our team. You're going, it's in two weeks. Here's the itinerary and list of things you'll need to get to participate." Guntz stated, handing me the paperwork. "Don't fight me on this, kid."

I nearly growled at his nickname for me, though I let it go. It's what I got for being the youngest on the team, it's what I deserved after delivering shitty games and making my team look like trash.

MIKA C.C.

When I knocked on Kallie's apartment door I wasn't expecting her to answer any faster than she always did, but maybe the days in between felt as slow and hard for her as they did for me, because she answered in a rush. I couldn't even greet her before her lips were on mine and I was carrying her to her room. We went from clothed to having both of our shirts off the second our bodies hit her bed. Her lips traveled down my chest kissing every tattoo, it was like being rewarded for every tattoo and every peak of skin in between. I had to hold Kallie's head just to get her to focus on me, so we could be eye to eye for at least a minute.

"Hey. I'm loving this, truly I am. But isn't there something we're missing here?" I asked, feeling something in me pump and I wasn't sure if it was my dick or my chest.

"Mood lighting?"

I chuckled, "How about letting *me* take control. I'm here to teach you, remember?"

"Sorry, I guess I got carried away since I hadn't gotten the chance to do anything with you earlier this week." I pushed her hair back to see the dimple in her smile. Letting my hand rest on the back of her neck.

"I've been anxious for this too. I've been hoping I could have my way with you. Show you how being touched isn't all about hard and fast."

Kallie's brows rose, " I just don't want to lose this feeling."

"Oh Princess, this feeling isn't going anywhere." I pulled her to me, our lips pressed hard together before her tongue seeks out mine. We made out until I got Kallie on her back with me on top of her. The look she gave me when I broke our kiss told me how responsive she was to my cock just pulsing in my jeans with her in between my legs.

"You think you'd be up for learning how to touch yourself tonight?" I asked with a wink, she nodded preemptively, as if she knew what I have coming for her, and I could only give her a quick smile before I kissed her again and distracted her from what's about to come.

Chapter 11

Kallie

I laid in bed with Jake towering over me as he promised to be gentle, as he explained that everything he's doing should feel good, and made me promise to tell him if something hurts. I nodded, not knowing what's to come, not when he asked me to pull off my pants, not when he asked me to spread my legs. It felt clinical for all of five seconds before Jake's mouth trailed down from my lips to my neck, and almost to my breasts. I couldn't help but let a small moan escape and it made him growl and look up at me.

Jake kept looking at me as he let his fingers trail down my chest down to my stomach before reaching the spot in between my legs. I tried to look away but I felt even more embarrassed than the times I've had my pap smears. I felt his hands grip my thighs before I finally looked at him as he stared back at me.

"What's wrong?" His eyebrows furrowed before he comes up to my eye level. "I haven't even done anything yet."

"I've never done this before and I'm a bit embarrassed…"

"So you want to stop?"

"I don't but I don't know how to fix it." I said with a little whine.

Jake looked at me with a curious gleam, "I think I might have something that might help." Jake got off the bed and disappeared from my room. I waited for almost a minute before he reappeared with his motorcycle helmet on.

He opened the visor to speak, but I stopped him, "Yes, close it. Now get over here." We're unable to kiss but it doesn't matter when his hands roam over my body, I couldn't help but react with a moan. When his fingers circled around a spot I didn't know existed I moaned louder, and when he entered a single finger inside me, I gasped. It's even more entertaining and sexier when I look at him and can see all the work his fingers do through the visor. Jake made me replace his hand with mine as I rubbed the same slow circles around myself. I heard him groan the more his one finger pumped in and out of me.

"So wet." He said with his voice muffled by the helmet, "So fucking tight." I moaned as I watched him finger me through the visor, his finger picked up the pace slightly and I felt myself tighten as he groaned again, "I feel you ready to come all over my finger, Princess." He starts to pull out as I moan but when he enters again I feel more pressure, with his second finger added.

"You feel that?" I asked through a moan.

"Yes, I can feel you holding back. Hold onto my fingers, Princess. Show me how badly you want to come."

I didn't know what he meant as I felt his fingers go deeper, I felt him start to pull back but pushed myself back down on his fingers.

"Fuck yes, Princess. Show me how much you love my fingers deep inside you." His fingers pulled away again as I thrusted myself further onto him. Jake kept making it happen and I'm nearly screaming from the feeling of his fingers doing something amazing to me. He continued to make me follow the fast rhythm until I felt the release, somehow different from before.

Jake didn't take off his helmet, instead he grabbed onto my thighs and pulled himself closer to me. I felt his dick in his pants, hard and pulsing... and wet?

"You feel this, Princess? This is what that pretty pussy of yours does to me. The more you come on my fingers, the more I'm going to come in my pants like a teenager. You're so fucking beautiful when you come, it's impossible for me to hold it in."

I'd lost my breath at his words when he stumbled to get up off the bed. He let me take off his helmet as I let myself stay in front of him half naked.

"You can put your clothes on now." Jake said giving me a once over as I hand him his helmet.

I shook my head lightly, "I just want you to stay with me right now. I'm not ready for my clothes just yet." Jake looked down at my lips just as I leaned to kiss him. I felt the heaviness of his helmet as it flopped on the bed, as I pulled him back down onto the bed with me until we do it all over again.

I spent a full two days letting Jake show me things about myself. After he taught me how to get myself off with my fingers, he then explored my erogenous zones, letting both of us discover where they were and how turned on I got by each of them. Almost all of my erogenous zones led to making Jake finger me until I orgasmed. While seven was the common answer from Monica Geller, the third did it for me. The back of my neck had been the spot that I enjoyed Jake the most. My thighs did as well, but something about his lips, his breath, his fingers and palm on my neck made everything in me weak for him.

Just walking past Jake in the middle of the work day was hard for me. Every time I saw his muscled body covered by his tight clothes working the field made me hot with need. It was hard for myself to believe that it had happened just like that. I was addicted, maybe it wasn't to Jake but to the feeling he gave me, the way he made me come, it was all I wanted, all I could think about. Even when I was trying to work in Nova's office, I kept looking out at the field empty or full and imagined Jake taking me on the mound and having his way with me. The daydream ended when Nova walked into her office.

"Oh my gosh, I'm so sorry." I said immediately standing from her chair.

"No, its fine." Nova waved her hand, "I'm not really back, I just have to pop in because I heard Jake is back. My dad said he's already doing better during games."

"What?" I asked with a head tilt.

"He said Jake had the yips, usually it's a mental thing. But I came back to see how much better he's been and this is honestly the best view to watch them play."

"Very true." I nodded, as we both looked out at the field to our team training. I had to hold any excitement back when I observed Jake do a baseball thing. I didn't major in sports, nor did I know too much about it, but I knew just enough for the job.

"God, why do their butts have to look so fucking good in those pants?" Nova sighed and waved a hand in her face.

I chuckled and looked at her. Nova's belly had grown quite a bit since the last time I saw her, she looked back at me with a smile.

"You down for another coffee date with Madison?"

I definitely felt the love every time I entered Curveballs, the cafe that Madison owned and ran. The first time I entered I was skeptical, imagining she had done it all from a marketing standpoint, but once I heard the full story it sent my heart into overdrive. Honestly, just listening to Madison talk about how long it took for her and Christian Hayes to get together just gave me hope that there was someone out there for everyone. Whether it was a friend who waited, or the right person wrong time or vice versa, it felt like a love story waiting to be told.

On my way back from the cafe, I called Jake hoping to catch him on his way home from work. It worked but not in the way I expected. As I waited for Jake to answer, I swore the motorcycle that drove past me was actually Jake's. I hadn't been able to tell right away until I sped up to recognize Jake's hoodie and his signature red helmet. By the time he picked up the phone I was already playing a kind of hide and seek game, since he hadn't seen my car behind him.

"Good afternoon, Princess Protection Program speaking." Jake had always found a funny or cute way to answer my calls and that had been his most frequent.

"I love that you think you're cute." I retorted back.

"What are you talking about? I am cute." Even with the Cardo in his helmet his voice still sounded a little muffled.

"Your butt is cute." I said, trying to be funny as I watch him swerve his bike from side to side. He definitely was in a goofy mood based on what I could tell from his driving.

"You know I'm staying home tonight, right? I don't have time to play cutesy with you." Jake said it like he's serious, just as a gust of wind blows up his shirt, showing off his back tattoos, including one that was lower than the rest.

"Right. You know, I never noticed you had more tattoos on your back."

"I have a bunch, those are my drunk tattoos. Can't see them, can't be mad, get it?"

"Oh so you know about your tramp stamp?"

"What are you even talking about?" He asked as he turned his head and noticed my car behind him. I waved with a smile, unsure if he can see me but hoping he can.

"You, Little Devil you." Jake joked, "Are you stalking me?"

"I wasn't until I saw the tramp stamp." I answered with a chuckle.

"It's not a tramp stamp."

"It's a tattoo on your lower back, a tramp stamp."

"I must've been drunk as hell. Take a pic next time." He said right as we pull up to a red light. It gave me the perfect chance to run up and snap a pic. Just as I pulled up his shirt to snap the picture, I give him the best gift a friend could give, I turned off his bike and ran for my car.

By the time I made it back in I watch Jake struggle to turn on his motorcycle for a minute past the light turning green and that makes him drive fast. Hoping he's still on the line I start to talk again.

"Don't go too fast, don't want a cop to catch you." I hesitated for a moment, thinking he hung up.

"It's not the cop I want to catch me." Jake said, it's then that I can hear the smile in his voice. "You gonna catch me, Little Devil or what?"

"Don't tease me with a good time Jake Rodgers." I answered back.

Whenever Jake came over to my apartment, all bets were off, it's the one and only place we could freely make-out in between him giving me lessons on sex. We've mastered fingering, clit-stimulating toy-play and vibrating insertion toys. More recently, had given the dry-humping and massaging his dick over his clothes, and so far, have successfully made him cream his pants more times than I can count.

The moment Jake comes into my apartment this time, I feel a chemical reaction. The feeling in my stomach never goes away when his eyes meet mine, but this felt raw, almost an unedited version of him I had yet to experience. Something I would have to instill into my memory. Jake moved straight for the bedroom as I followed him. There's no make out session, no pure animalistic humping, just him giving me orders and I obeyed every single one, as I got completely naked for him.

I watched as Jake moved my mirror closer to the bed, he read my confused expression plain and simple.

"Remember how we talked about how hard it is for you to know when you're about to come?"

"Yeah." I answered hesitantly.

"It's time you learn the moment it's about to happen." He sounds so raw with his words, almost like he's been waiting for this, like he's been planning this one the longest. Something about his voice turns me on more.

Jake shuts the door and drew in the curtains, then walked over to me and pulled up my chin, "Princess, promise me that no matter what happens after tonight we'll still be friends."

"Friends with benefits." I answered him with a smile and wink. He kissed me softly before we start, and what seems like any other time we've done this before. It's when he gets off the bed that I'm confused. From the mirror I can see him on his knees, my legs sprawled wide open for him, but when I look at his face I see the glint in his eyes.

Jake's fingers play with my clit just long enough that my pussy starts to feel warm and damp, he let his other hand's fingers slide inside me as I started to feel the build up of his second finger. Every time he entered his second, I felt a little uneasy at first but get used to it quickly after. This time it didn't hurt, and when the build up came I expect to look in the mirror and see him the way I did when he first fingered me. This is different, I watched as he pulled out his fingers from inside me, I watched as he added a third finger and I nearly screamed out his name.

"Is that feeling good?" Jake whispered.

"So much pressure, but so far so good."

"Do you feel close yet?" He asked as his fingers pumped in and out of me. I shook my head as I looked down at him. "Didn't think so." He moaned as he continued filling me with his fingers.

I'm wondering what the next part is when he pulled his fingers out and sucked them into his mouth. I observed as Jake inhaled and exhaled before he pulled the fingers out of his mouth.

"Ah fuck, how did I know you'd taste so fucking good?"

I moaned at his words, unsure of how his fingers in his mouth turned me on. Part of me wanted to respond but he cuts me off when he looks up at me, our eyes locking.

"I'm going to devour you tonight, princess. Is that okay?" Jake asked. I nodded just barely knowing the basics of what was about to happen. Not when he took the longest lick of my pussy, licking me from top to bottom.

"Fuck fuck fuck," I moaned the words as he does it three more times.

"I've not even started yet." He whispered before I feel his mouth suck on my clit. Jake's exhale caused me to moan from the sensitivity. "God, I'm gonna feast on this pussy, you hear me, Princess? I'm going to lick every last bit of you but not before I show you what you look like when you come the first time."

"The first time?" I questioned a moment too late as his tongue digs into my pussy, lapping and licking me in a way I hadn't known possible. His tongue intensified and I felt my pussy clench around him. My pelvis thrusted the more his tongue darted inside me and I couldn't help but moan and try to find something stronger than my bed sheets to hold onto.

It's when Jake looked up at me with his tongue circling and licking my clit that he grabbed my hands and shoved them both into my hair. "Hold onto me," he whispered into my skin, before his tongue darts back out to get me closer to the edge. I pulled on his hair the longer his tongue stayed there, feeling the pulse of my pussy, the sensitivity of my body reacting under him.

Jake added a finger the more his tongue focused on my clit and then another when he knew I could take more. And I'm right on the edge when I shouted out for him.

"I feel it!" I clenched further around his fingers as they curled and pumped. Jake didn't pull his head away just simply breathes a word of something against my clit.

"Focus on the mirror."

I forced myself up to look as I watched this tattooed and muscled man, down on his knees, treating my pussy like it's his last meal. I felt the pump of his fingers and tongue at the same time and that's when I toppled over, when I felt my orgasm. Jake removes his fingers and moves his head to the side to watch my cum seep out of me.

"That's my fucking good girl, look at that pussy shine," He whispered at me from the mirror. I looked down at him the moment he looked up at me. Jake pulled himself over me, "Now I'm gonna have you the way I really want to." I sighed before his mouth dropped down on mine. Our kiss held there before he pushed his tongue in my mouth so I taste myself, it's a taste I've never imagined but it's soon replaced by the taste of him and I enjoy his tongue for a moment later until Jake folded himself off of me.

I get a moment to really look at him as I watch him move the mirror to another side of the bed. Not only is this sexy man teaching me, he's showing me and I'm not sure I could ever want it to stop. Jake and I have the perfect set up, we get along and yet can bug each other endlessly and can mess around in my bed while staying mostly professional at work. A friends with benefits situation I would never let go of, especially when I look lower and see the tent in his pants. The gray sweatpants do nothing to hide his bigger than normal sized cock and I am glad he's slowly getting me to that point, but also makes me wonder if we ever will get to the point of actual sex.

The moment I'm ready to ask, Jake is back on his knees as he looked up at me. "I didn't say you could sit up. Lay back down, Princess. Unless you need to use the bathroom, I'm the only thing that matters right now." He lightly pushed me back down, with his hands wrapped around my breasts as he began to feast on me again. I moaned as I looked up and see the mirror and when I gaze down at him, Jake is looking at the mirror as he tongue fucks me. It's a crazy sight to be seen, but then he rolls his tongue like a Spanish 'r' and my eyes roll at the back of my head.

It's not until the fifth time I've orgasmed that Jake comes up for air. The mess all over his face is the single most hottest thing I've seen of a man's face. I've never felt so content before, never felt so wanted with the way Jake's green eyes stare back at me. We share a long kiss where he met me on the bed and with heavy eyelids, I fell asleep practically in his arms.

I woke up the next morning to Jake nowhere in my bed, it's almost a sad feeling, but I don't let it affect me too much when it's not been a discussed topic between us. When I got out of bed I immediately found Jake's riding sweater and put it on. It's not meant to mean anything but I can't help but imagine what it would be like to wake up next to him, to wear his clothes when he'd be at an away game. By the time I make it out to the kitchen Cherry is whining from her kennel. I go to let her out but noticed a note on the coffee table before I do, I picked it up to read Jake's scribbled note

> *Out to get coffee, don't you dare be wearing clothes when I get back ;)*

I chuckled just as a knock comes from my door.

Figuring the person at the door is Jake, I checked myself in the reflection of my tv, I pat my hair down with my hands and fingers and make sure the sweater hides my thighs. Once I made it over to the door, I played with my hair for another moment before I open it.

"Lane!" I shouted, completely busted, unaware and looking ten times worse in front of my brother. If he were to put two and two together just by the sweater...

"Hey sis! Just wanted to check on things, it's been a few weeks since just you and I talked. I heard from Nova that you've become good friends with Madison, which is super rare for her, because she's had the same friends forever."

"Ha, yeah. Madison and I are actually supposed to hang out sometime today." I lied, hoping my brother would get the hint and leave before Jake got back.

"Have you girled up my apartment yet?" Lane asked as a joke, it's a pretty lame attempt at getting me to talk about my decor skills, which have been pretty nonexistent since Bruce ruined everything I bought.

"Oh, not too much. A little here and there." I answered with a shrug.

"Is there a reason why you're not inviting your brother in?" Lane's brows turn and I'm a little put-off by his request to come in, but I can't deny him when it's his apartment. I opened the door wider for him letting him come in. I almost close the door, just leaving it ajar for when Jake would come back.

"Who's that?" My brother stated, pointing to Cherry.

"My dog."

"That is not the dog I gifted you."

"Well the thing is…" I almost trail off as the door opened as my brother continued.

"I got you a bigger dog, right? Pretty sure his name was Bruce. And this dog does not look like a 'Bruce'. I'm not even sure that thing is a dog."

Jake stayed behind Lane with a smug look on his face, as the more my brother talks Jake mimicked him. I tried not to smile as my eyes trained on Jake for a minute too long, Lane looked over his shoulder before he turned to get a better look at his best friend.

"Hey. What are you doing here?" Lane's brows furrowed though the start of a smile peeked through.

"Oh you know, doing my due diligence." Jake answered with a shrug, he glanced at me with a quick wink before he dropped down to grab an excited Cherry.

"What–"

"Taking this little girl to the vet, she has an appointment to get spayed." Jake said with a convincing lie.

Lane's eyes shifted to me, "Why is my best friend taking your dog to a vet appointment? And where is the dog I got you?"

"First of all, you being a grown man calling another grown man your best friend is still weird. Jake is doing me a favor since I was just called into the office. And second, Bruce was kind of vicious, no offense, but he was kind of scary." I explained it all, quick and simple, that I hope it doesn't bring any other kind of interrogation from my foster brother but his eyes turn to slits and that's when I knew he's just getting started.

"Where's the dog, Kallie?" Lane asked with a rough edge to his voice that made me gulp. I had never had trouble lying to my brother before, it was easy over the phone for the few years we'd been living in different states, but with him towering over me, I feel myself waiver. Coming up with a lie on the spot is way easier when my brother's eyes aren't directly on me with his voice turning into a boiling burn I've only heard a handful of times, and never directed towards me before. There's a deep silence between us as my mouth opens and closes, I stuttered out a vowel.

"Does she need to explain herself more than once, Lane? She said the dog wasn't right for her, plain and simple." Jake doesn't sound an inch of angry, genuine patience is the only thing I see behind his eyes when he winked at me.

"Thank you." I mouthed to him before my brother passed a look between the both of us.

"Okay, fine. I guess. I still think it's kind of messed up –" My brother's tone back to normal gave me my voice back.

93

"We– I didn't give Bruce back to the pound if that's what you're worried about. I found a home for him with Hughes."

"Hughes?" My brother's brows danced in question.

"Dude always wanted a dog." Jake answered him, finally picking up Cherry from the floor.

"I guess..." Lane said as I shrugged back at him in reply. Jake excused himself from our conversation as he casually walked out of my apartment with Cherry in his arms. I extended my hand to push my brother out the door, as I start to leave my own apartment. Lane glared.

"So this – Jake taking your dog is – what?"

"A friend helping a friend?" My answer turned into a question. Even I couldn't believe my lie, let alone try to consider Jake my friend. Friends didn't do the kind of thing we were doing.

Lane hummed, "Interesting. But I'm not actually mad about it. I'm glad you've found a couple friends outside of me and Nova, just um. Weird to choose my best friend."

I rolled my eyes at him.

"Fine. My *good* friend. Just don't let him get away with hitting on you. Jake will assume you actually want to fuck him if you let him go on and on."

I let out a honk of a laugh, not even a full single laugh, just a random 'ha' sound. As if I didn't already know the way Jake eye-fucked me, the way he looked at me when I touch myself in front of him and not to mention what happened the previous night...

"Yeah, don't you worry, bro. I am keeping him in the friend zone." I said through a forced smile. If my brother dared to look a little closer he'd probably see the panic behind my eyes.

"*Good.* Good job." Lane puts his hand on top of my head and ruined my hair.

"What the- you're ruining my effortless look! Do you know how long it took me to make my hair look like this?"

"I'd assume less than a minute since it's effortless–" Lane joked.

"Does Nova teach you anything about women at her place?"

Lane's grin picked up at that question, it didn't take me long to figure out what he's thinking of, my face rings with disgust.

"Never mind, don't tell me. Gross, I do not want to know what Nova teaches you."

He chuckled, "Just to spare you the details, I won't, but I am thinking about them right now."

I groaned, "Thanks for that. Now I have to go to work with that being our last conversation."

By the time Lane is out of my hair, Jake comes back with the coffee and Cherry and I don't know which one of them to hug first. I had to stress myself just to get Lane out the door and pretend to drive to work, which was me just driving two blocks and back to avoid Lane noticing my car. So the second I see coffee I lunge for Jake.

"Thank you thank you thank you." I say kissing his cheeks and then once on the lips.

"If your thank yous are always like that I've got a better place for you to kiss." Jake says with a wide smile. I nearly smack him with the coffee, but it's from Madison's and I can't waste good coffee quite like that.

"You're lucky I have a cup of coffee in my hands and not a shoe." I respond as I walk my ass back into my apartment.

"Is that my sweater?" Jake asked before Cherry followed us into the apartment. He closed the door, "Wow, either way because I want to do bad things to you in it."

I take a sip of my coffee, "Easy there, Ghost Rider, last night wasn't enough for you?"

Jake crowds my space, "I could eat and slurp you up for every meal of the day." His green eye winks at me and I nearly fold right there. I'm sure he can see the redness on my face, but he doesn't say a damn thing about it.

Instead I grab a piece of my hair and twirl it, "So what are your plans for the day? I assume not camping out here for the rest of the day." I watch as he takes a long sip of his coffee.

When he sets his coffee down on the counter, I see his eyes wide, "Shit. I have to pack for that damn camping trip in three days."

"Oh fuck, me too!"

"What do you mean, you too? You're going?"

"Nova and her stupidly cute pregnant belly aren't allowed to camp. It's half of the reason why Lane came by this morning, to ask if I could take over her spot as a supervisor. She was supposed to do it with her dad..."

"Coach Guntz is coming too?" Jake groans, "Shit, now I actually have to go and participate."

"So what? He's not going to bite."

"No, but he's been on my ass all season."

"The yips, right?" I ask, scratching my head, pretending I don't know.

"Yeah. How do you know about that? You're not even a sports fan."

"The office talks." I say with my arms out wide.

"Or Nova because her dad tells her everything, and she only has two friends to tell things to."

I put my hand to my chest, almost offended for her, "For one, that is my sister in law, do not be rude. And two, she is such a chisme! I think the mom thing changed her."

"Lane's changed so it wouldn't surprise me one bit." Jake adds in, and it almost sounds like he's jealous of Lane.

I try not to chuckle, "Whatever they won't be at the *wilderness retreat* with us."

"It's a glorified team building retreat for the misfits of our team."

"Yeah, I tried to make it sound better." I replied, nearly gulping the last of my coffee.

"The good news." Jake says as he takes the cup of coffee from my hands and puts it on the counter, "is that we both will be there. We can share a tent, maybe have a fun group activity just me and you?"

"Jake," I pause with a sigh, "We'll be out with like five other teammates, I'm not really sure I want them seeing us like that."

"You'd rather them see you as the only woman there? Or maybe you just want one on one action with another teammate?"

I feel my eyes roll from a mile away, "Not that we're anything outside of a beneficial friendship, but even if I wanted to hook up with another guy there, I wouldn't."

"Right so if ZX10RZaddy was there, you wouldn't hook up with him?"

I gasped, "Don't you dare throw my instagram crush in that line up!"

"I mean, sure he's good looking, but he's not as good looking as me." Jake says with confidence. I let my shoulders fall. "Right?" Jake's glare at me intensified, "Right?!"

I chuckle, "Yes of course, Jake. You can be my Zaddy." I feign a sexy voice.

"I mean, hell, I let you become my backpack and you're ready to leave me for a BikerGram creator."

The eyeroll I give him is loud, "You're so dramatic, Jake." I say as I walk off to the bedroom stripping off his sweater.

"That's Ghost Rider to you!" Jake yells right before running after me.

Chapter 12

Jake

Two days before the trip, I spent another night worshipping Kallie's pussy. It was honestly the best tasting pussy in my entire life of eating pussies. A drug I couldn't quit, and Kallie knew it. I had gotten to the point where I had stopped caring if I came in my fucking pants, because I was having the time of my life teaching Kallie all about sex, all about what I could give her.

It was this night also that I was teaching Kallie about blow jobs, a night I should've been able to enjoy. As much as I wanted her to get on her knees for me, I knew it was impossible. I knew Kallie would do it and try to enjoy it but the truth was, I had a pierced dick, a Jacob's Ladder. Quite literally I got the piercings once I knew they were named after me, because I believed that I had the same name as the piercing for a reason. And I did, I used my dick for good and fucked women that had experienced multiple dicks or guys with piercings. I loved finding a woman who knew what it was like before. I wouldn't put Kallie through that, a regular dick was already going to be a stretch for her, but to add my piercing to it, it would be harder, rougher especially for her first time. Instead I had Kallie use toys and phallic foods to suck on, which, bad news for me, made me come inside my pants for the hundredth time.

Then the next morning came and as gorgeously swollen her lips were, with the aquamarine of her eyes shining, I thought for sure she was about to let me down gently. I really thought with her most perfect expression that it meant the worst was coming. Turned out it was a different kind of worse.

Kallie broke down to me, swearing that all of her crappy horrible memories were replaced by what I had done for her, but it didn't stop her from telling me all about them. About the foster-dad that tried to fuck her when he'd come home drunk, about a different foster-brother that threw bottles at her when she wore any clothes that showed her skin. And about the jerk ex that not only assaulted her, but then cheated on her and stole her personal belongings. I thought she was done but then she added more – the whole reason why she moved to Florida. A reason that was too terrible to think about. I had thought my parents were on the wrong side of life but after hearing what Kallie's birth parents did to her, I wished she had a chance to experience a normal life with parents.

If none of that was enough, Kallie wanted to make sure I knew that she didn't deserve the title of Princess, because of everything she had been through. So many times I had seen her face turn over the nickname, but now it all made sense. It didn't fit her personality, this whole time she let it slide because she knew I enjoyed it, but she thought she wasn't that. That she was unworthy of being treated like a Princess. And if I could change that, I would, but for her I would embrace it. At least for a little while...

Before the crappy camping trip with my teammates, I had this crazy idea. It had been ridiculous and felt like something a boyfriend would do, but with Kallie and I being our own team it felt right. Kallie had ridden on my motorcycle more than three times and each time I felt like she loved it more and more. Hell, she loved wearing my sweater so much I let her keep that, so it didn't feel too off-brand for me to do something like, buy her a custom made helmet. Nothing was really out of my price range, so it didn't feel too big of a gift, but I wanted to give it to her before the trip, wanted to give her the option to deny it, or accept it and ride to the campground in style with me.

Was it a stupid idea to make Kallie a helmet with devil horns? Nowhere I looked online had a customizable tiara or crown on it, and I was still torn over the rebrand of her nickname. She'd always be Princess, but there had been her alter ego, her biker girl persona, her quick wit, the way she begged me to teach her, the way she'd get naked just for me. The Little Devil she was, whether she believed that one too, was up for debate, but I needed her to know that she would always have a part of me.

Kallie answered the door in my sweatshirt, it had been the third time I'd seen her wear it around her apartment and it was cute as fuck. If I had any sense of mind, I would've said screw the benefits and just let her have me. But she was too cute, too pure-hearted for me.

"Hey, what's up?" Her voice sounded so chipper, like she'd been up for hours and was just waiting for something good to happen for the day. I assumed she noticed I was hiding something behind my back before she even said anything, but with the biggest frog in my throat I revealed the helmet to her.

"Wanna go for a ride, Little Devil?" I asked as I watched the smile grow on her face.

"This is so great! Is this really just for me?"

"No one else." I answered, trying not to answer with my cheesy line. *No one else could fall from Heaven and hurt for so long without a drop of affection. Yes, Little Devil, it's yours.*

Tears welled in Kallie's eyes but she shoved them away with a knuckle, "You're the best friend anyone could ever ask for, you know that?" She hugged me while holding her helmet.

Once I let go of her, I let her get changed for the ride and paid some attention to the other little lady of the house.

"Hey Jake!" Lane called from the other side of the field. I looked towards him as I carried my gear.

"Hey, aren't you supposed to be home with Nova?" I asked with an accusatory voice. Already annoyed that it was him and Nova that set this camp thing up and neither of them could follow through on it themselves.

"Yeah, I'm actually about to go. I just wanted to say, thanks for being so cool with Kallie. I hope it's no hard feelings but I just can't have you dating my little sister. I know you have said you changed, and

I feel like I've seen a lot of change from you. I like to assume you being friends with Kallie did that, but I wanted to give you a heads up that I'm still not comfortable with it. The friendship I can barely get my head around, ya know? It's just a –"

I cut him off before he could get all high and mighty on me, "That's great, Lane. I'm glad you came to tell me that. And not anything else. You know I really hope you and Nova are happy together." I turned to walk away but Lane put a hand on my shoulder.

"What's that supposed to mean?" He asked as I turned back around, "I'm just trying to protect her."

"Maybe it's not Kallie that needs protecting, have you ever thought of that? She can handle herself pretty well from what I've seen. And if it bugs you so much, then tell her that too, not just me." I looked him up and down, "You know I keep calling you my best friend, but lately you've been so far up your own ass that you haven't got a clue what's gone on in mine. Did you even bother to ask me how my grandpa was? Have you ever even looked at the date to see my parents' death dates just recently passed? No you haven't. And normally I wouldn't even care, but you know who did ask how I was? Who did ask how my grandpa was? Your sister. And you know why I have to go on this stupid thing? Because my best friend couldn't cover my ass or have my back when I was playing a shitty game! What happened, Lane? You said you wanted to be a hitter, and then you're just gone! You only show up when it comes to protecting someone who can protect themselves. So I'm gonna say this once, don't come at me again over shit I can't control. Find another best friend."

I walked away with not much else to say. I packed my bag into Kallie's trunk as she sat in her car waiting for me. I didn't even bother looking back because I knew Lane was looking anywhere but at me. If I had it my way, I could *maybe* be with a girl like Kallie and not have to deal with her self-absorbed brother ever again.

Chapter 13

Kallie

The camping trip had been planned long before Jake and I started up but the second the date came closer, was the moment I started freaking out. I couldn't freak out to Nova and certainly not my brother. What was worse was Lane actually considering joining us. His reason was that it was him and Nova who had set it up for the problem teammates and he wanted to oversee it himself. I had to figure out a way around it, a way for him not to come. Jake being one of the problem teammates was also not helpful, especially with him whispering to me every other night that he couldn't wait to share a tent. I had to break it to Jake that I bought my own and hoped to get it up without help from anyone.

It took until the next work day to convince Lane not to attend the camping trip and it was only successful thanks to Coach Guntz walking in on our conversation and him offering up his service to oversee the group with me, so all of it had been worked out in my favor. Or in Jake's favor…

"It's not weird that I'm coming with, right?" I asked him as we hike up to our campsite. I couldn't help but feel that little knot in my stomach as I swallowed my question. It hadn't been weird between us so far, but I kept on thinking the more we're together with the team, the more they'll pick up on what's happening between me and Jake.

"Nah. What's a little fun between us and five other teammates?"

"Ha. There's no way I'm sleeping in a tent with you or any of the others. That'll give them the wrong impression."

"Who?" Jake asked with a smirk.

"What?"

"It'll give *who* the wrong impression?"

I made a face, "Everyone. I mean, no one needs to know about us, right?"

"I guess–"

"Well let's keep it that way. Neither of us need it to get back to my brother."

Jake rolled his eyes at me, "Fair. But that doesn't mean I have to like it."

"You think I'm going to like it?" I asked about the camping.

"You'll be surrounded by hot men who wear tight pants. How could you not like it?"

I shrugged and looked him up and down, "I mean, I got my hot pants guy right here."

I heard Jake sigh, "Good answer."

Only a few hours after arriving did the guys set up their tents. Coach Guntz happily set up mine for me without me having to ask. It had been a sweet thing for him to do, especially with me being the only woman on the trip. I finally got why everyone said baseball was a man's job, but that didn't stop me from trying to make it a woman's. If I had stayed in North Carolina I would've been surrounded by more women, but I had to be happy here, I had to try and make it work.

Once night fell, we started the campfire, ate hotdogs and marshmallows over the fire. It was easy and nice, but I was kind of scare–

"Scary story time?" Zack asked, giving everyone a look.

Exactly three of us gave him a scary story, none of which were scary to say the least. Then, of course, Guntz told one that happened in the park we were in.

Everyone went off to bed after the campfire went out, everyone but Jake and Zack. Both looked at me like I was going to be the one to send them to bed. Instead, I gave Jake a look and he gave me a nod to walk with him towards—where I didn't know. I quickly got to my feet the moment Jake stood and yawned. It was hard to believe it was real with the loud sound emanating from his mouth, but I took it as face value.

I didn't have to say anything to Jake or Zack before we started walking the same way, Zack still sitting near the campfire, the glitters of the fire going out as he sat looking up to no good.

"I'm pretty sure he's got a thing for you. And here I was believing you when you said no guys look at you." Jake said with a smirk.

"Zack? Nah, nope, no way. We're friends, friendly, he's a sweetheart to me." The high pitched tone of my voice rising.

"Relax, Kallie." He chuckled, "it's fine. We're not really together and if you want to find out if there's anything there, now would be the night. No one will bat an eye at the noises in a campground, it's where everyone gets freaky."

"Really?" My voice changed.

"Look at you, little devil. You sound like you are interested in him."

I blushed, grateful the darkness hides the color of my skin, "I wouldn't say that–"

Jake's grin stopped me as he began to turn me back to the campfire, "Now's your chance to put what you've learned to use, little devil. Get you some." He said, whispering the words into my ears before he playfully smacked my ass sending me forward with two steps.

"Hey Zack."

It took a little conversation between us before Zack told me he'd been eyeing me for a while. It was a weird start, but I had to say, I was humbled and partially turned on. Zack was one of the more popular players that didn't act like a player, though he did have a temper. Every time I had talked to Zack in the past I could see his attraction towards me and I had the littlest crush on him back. So being alone in the woods with him wasn't exactly bad, but without Jake's encouraging words in my ears, I kept on wishing a bear would growl or make a brief appearance.

It wasn't until we were on the topic of our brief attraction that Zack made a move, it was a quick kiss, but the yearning feeling of my pussy didn't go away. I was half-sure I needed to make the next move but the fire did it for me when it burnt out. I held onto Zack, hoping he could see better in the dark than I could. Turned out my move wasn't the greatest, but got us to making out on a log before he took off his shirt and I got to feel Hemsworth level muscles.

Zack wasn't the one I wanted to be my first, but it was obvious Jake didn't want to be my first. So between the circumstances and the place I was stuck in, I chose Zack. It only took us three positions before he came and that's when I realized, I fucked up. He was the exact kind of guy that got what he wanted and left, the definition of the kind of guy I didn't want, had taken my first time. But weirdly, he didn't feel like my first time, Zack didn't feel like anything to me, maybe that's how Jake had felt all those times with all those other women. I felt empty and missing the one person who made me feel like—like a fucking Princess...

Chapter 14

Jake

Sleep evaded me the longer I thought about what Kallie was doing, if she was fucking Zack or if they were just fooling around. The jealousy that pooled in my stomach was nothing compared to the idea that I didn't get the chance to sink my cock into her pretty pussy first. I never wanted to be a girl's first time, I didn't want Kallie to be subjected to me specifically because of my piercings, I didn't want her to be turned off or worried that it would hurt even more. I had no true idea how it felt for women, yet alone one's first time, but just imagining someone's first time with a pierced dick was a whole other thought. I thought I was doing a good deed not taking Kallie's virginity, that it wouldn't be me hurting her on her first time.

Never did I think that I'd be worried for someone other than myself, yet alone a woman who was way out of my league and one that I'd consider my friend. Who knew a friends with benefits situation would lead me here, would lead me to the idea of competing for getting to have her first. At least I had taken enough of her firsts, but just knowing that Kallie was getting railed by another didn't make me feel any better. It should've been my dick, even if I knew mine would possibly hurt her, I could've gone slow, I could've taken my time and found a way to make it pleasurable for both of us.

Even as I laid in my tent my thoughts drift to if I set myself up for this life; a life alone, where no matter how close to a person I could get, I will always push them away or always feel alone in their presence. A feeling that I had yet to experience with Kallie, but I knew in time it would happen, if she didn't find a person better for her, first. I'd never be the better option for a girl like her, yet alone the kind of guy that any woman would settle for. Just the thought of it had me reconsidering the situation I'd put myself in. Her name in my head rang as I tried to forget my recurring thoughts and stroked my cock. It wasn't even a minute later that I heard the rustle and zipper of the entrance of my tent that Kallie materialized in front of me. Her hair looked a mess and her shirt looked stretched out from the way it hung off her shoulder.

"Did I wake you?" She asked before I shook my head, my hand stilled.

"Hey. How was it?" I asked, refusing to take my hand off my cock, even under the sleeping bag there was no way she knew. My sweet innocent princess wasn't so innocent anymore but I knew she thought more of me.

"It was – He was good. Nice might be a better word." She answered, trying not to look me directly in the eyes.

"Nice isn't bad for your first time." I said, as if I'd learned the heavy details. Did he finger her until she came? Did he taste her on his tongue before his dick did?

"Yeah." Kallie shrugged and I could feel the uncertainty in the air, that there's something she's not saying.

"Princess," is the only word I need to use to get her to look at me.

"He didn't – I mean, I didn't..." She groaned, "I can't look at you and explain this."

"Try. What did he do, what didn't he do?" I asked with a brow raised, as I sat up.

"Jake–" Kallie said with a whine.

"Did he touch you?"

"Yes."

"Where?" I asked, finally removing my hand from my cock, "demonstrate. Use my hand."

Taking my hand, she placed my palm on her breast. "Here and..." She does the same with my other hand but instead of placing it on her breast, placed it between her thighs. "Here."

"Did he do this over your clothes or under?"

"Both." She answered, looking me in the eye.

"And it wasn't, it didn't get you off?"

"I– um. He *isn't* you."

My cock pulsated at her words as a beat of silence passed between us before my lips crashed into hers. Both of us fumbling off our shirts like she didn't just lose her virginity an hour ago.

Out of breath, Kallie spoke, "Fuck, Jake. This doesn't seem – weird?"

"Do you want to stop?"

"No, god no. I just don't know the rules, is it bad to want to fuck you after I just lost my virginity to someone else?"

Her question rang in my ear for a second longer before I finally answered, "No. Fuck no. You're not with him, you're not with me, but if you feel uncomfortable—"

"I don't. I just don't want you to feel like I'm a..."

"That's not a problem with me, Princess. I don't think any less of you, if anything, I want more of you. I want you to show me what he did so I can show you how much better I am."

Kallie's lips fell back on mine for a moment, "Why does that turn me on even more?"

"Because you know how rewarding my tongue can be." I said kissing her again.

"You may be right." Kallie agreed with a chuckle.

Not even a minute later are my hands back in the same spots he touched, fingering her one finger at a time until she's moaning my name. I smiled as my lips press along her neck, with the knowledge she's already forgotten about fuck-face and my dick hasn't even sunk inside her yet. By the time I started inching a third finger Kallie pulled back with an exhale.

"Only two." She said, her eyes met with mine and I noticed the reluctance behind them.

"If you want me to be inside you, I'm gonna need to add another finger, princess. Can you handle that?"

Kallie sucked in a breath, "Yes."

"Good girl." I answered back as I eased my finger to the knuckle. "You're so fucking tight." I said as I felt her pussy pulsate around my fingers.

"Do I," She paused, "Do I need to be worried that you'll be too big?"

With my free hand I pushed the hair out of her face, and shook my head slightly, "I promise you a perfect fit, my cock might just be a bit different from Zack's."

Her expression turned scared, "How different can yours be?"

"Piercings..."

"What? How many?"

"You can count for yourself, princess." I smirked back at her.

"Jake!" She shouted before I press my mouth onto her lips to shush her. My fingers curled and pumped into her. Kallie moaned as I fucked her with my fingers until I felt the explosion of her come down my hand. Every time I felt her orgasm it felt even better than the last and I can't wait to feel it all over my cock.

After making out with Kallie for what felt like a full hour, I finally got her into a position where her leg wrapped around my shoulder as my fingers drew further into her pussy. Kallie finally felt the hardness of my cock still in my briefs against her ass as my fingers pulled out of her. She looked up at me as I sucked each finger clean of her sweet orgasms, a taste I would never get tired of, Kallie looks entranced the longer my tongue focuses on each finger. It wasn't until I stopped completely that I feel her hand pull at my boxers, just barely pulling them down. I smirked and looked at her.

"You Little Devil, can't wait any longer, can you?" I asked as her head shook from side to side. I helped her out and pulled them down, as my cock bounced out of the elastic. Kallie's jaw dropped, if I wasn't up for recreating her first time, I'd have her on her knees before I'd enter that throbbing, persistent pussy of hers. I swore the longer she

114

looked at it, my cock grew harder and I'm betting she's counting the five piercings from tip to base.

"I don't think I can wait any longer," Kallie said with a slight whimper to her voice, I swallowed and inched toward her. She's so fucking beautiful, laying naked on my cot with that look of need written on her face. I didn't want to question why we'd wait another minute for this, why I would when I've wanted this the whole time.

"Condom?" I asked with a brow raised. Whatever thought that encouraged me to ask, stopped me from moving any further.

"Um. I used one with him, but I am on birth control. It's not necessary."

"Right, I knew that," I shook my head with my response, I started to move again.

"Jake?" I looked at her as she used my name as a question, "Are you nervous?" Kallie's little smirk with that question made me gain my sense of self back.

I let out a breath, "No. Not with you."

"Then why are you so far?" The question seemed so silly when I look down and see the tip of my cock just brushing the lips of her pussy. I chuckled as I bent down and kissed that smirk off Kallie's face and just as I do I thrust myself little by little into her.

The moans that come from Kallie almost sounded unrealistic, I had heard so many women's voices when I entered them before, but none of them compare to the sounds that come from my princess.

"Not hurting, right?" I asked after the first part of the ladder enters her.

Kallie exhaled, "God, no. It feels–" I watched her eyes roll back, "So fucking amazing."

No one else's explanation of my cock will ever compare to those three words from her mouth.

"Jake, more." It's all I need to push more of me inside her, she repeated it until my dick is fully inside of her. It's then that I gazed at her and see how much Kallie has enjoyed every second and I've barely begun fucking her. Then she opened her eyes and I pumped my cock slowly to build up to a decent rhythm.

By the time I'm fucking her like I want, at a comfortable speed for both of us and in a hard but pleasurable way for her, I felt her pussy grip and explode all over my cock. Her orgasm nearly brought me to coming inside her, but I keep my speed up and work her until hers passes, and as it did I had to pull out as I felt myself unable to hold onto my own. The smell of our sex settled in the tent, but the second she looked at me, she gazed down at my hand, full of my cum.

"I'll go clean up real quick." I started to back up, but she adjusted herself and grabbed my forearm.

"Let me." Kallie doesn't give me a second to respond as she pulled my hand closer to her face. I watched in disbelief as the woman I've been calling princess, licked my hand clean of our mixed cum. My eyes followed down to her throat watching it bob as she swallowed it all, and her expression doesn't even look displeased by the taste. Out of every experience I've had, it's the sexiest thing I've ever had and it almost makes me instantly hard.

"Little Devil." I whispered, as my hand wrapped around her neck and lightly brought her closer to me until our lips met, our tongues tangle as I taste both of us in her mouth, as I licked her tongue. Kallie moaned in between our lips and it's literally the only thing that does me in and gets me to fuck her a second time.

Chapter 15

Kallie

The last two days of our camping trip had been spent getting the five team members and Jake to do team building exercises. Coach Guntz and I watched as they completed a geocaching scavenger hunt, a hide and seek game to find three baseballs in the forest, and another where each pair had to find a large branch and carve it to resemble a baseball bat. There had been other less fun activities but I couldn't help but laugh out loud when Jake and Nick were paired up to catch two fish and what they came back with were the smallest anchovy sized fish.

I had only been camping once before and it was when I was a little kid, so getting the chance to reclaim another bad memory made me feel even better about myself. Starkey Park had been a ways off our map, but it had been far enough from St. Pete that no one would suspect a major league baseball team would be out camping. The campground was huge and the nights we spent in front of the campfire were my favorite, even with Guntz yelling at us how to roast marshmallows the correct way.

The last night of the trip was spent in my own tent fifty feet away from Jake's and the longer I lied in my one-person sleeping bag, was the longest time I had been alone in months. I didn't even realize it, but Jake had become such an influence on my life, he'd become someone important to me. Jake had proven that he felt I was important too, with Cherry and the helmet made just for me, but it felt like lately the more he and I shared, the closer we became, and I wasn't even referring to the sex. I just had the hope that whatever it was between us wouldn't ruin the friendship we built.

After the long weekend away, I stopped by Madison's cafe on the way to pick up Cherry from Nova's and hoped my two friends would greet me with a happy face and some good advice. However, that was not the case when I walked into the cafe. I sat at the bar as I waited for my coffee order and it was when Madison came out with a grumpy look on her face that I realized something was wrong.

"What happened?" I asked, nearly having to grab Mads hand for her to pay attention to me. She had been so distracted and in her own element that I wasn't sure she'd stop to recollect her thoughts.

"Lane disappeared."

My eyes grew wide, "What?"

"I guess he was too on edge between the new baby and some other shit, but he's been gone since you guys left. I'm not even sure he left Nova a note as far as I know. So I've been over at her place helping her the last few days and man, I understand his reasoning to leave, but he has a fucking family. Everyone's been pretty pissed." Madison explained with a crease in her brows.

"Does Nova's dad know?" I asked, feeling the pounding of my heart.

"I doubt it, if you just found out from me, it's possible she hasn't said a thing to him yet."

"I should go talk to Nova, then." I let go of Madison's hand to grab my coffee.

"Before you do, please make her eat this. She's been running on fumes and I know she hasn't eaten today since I haven't been there." Madison handed me a to-go bag, "It's a baseball shaped cronut. There's a few in there if you want one."

I nodded just barely holding in my tears. Aggravated that my brother left his pregnant wife alone to take care of their baby. I could barely stomach the thought of Lane just leaving, he'd considered Nova his world, Quinn his everything, something just didn't add up.

I spent a half hour cleaning up Nova's living room as she sat on the couch and cried for the tenth time since I arrived. Between Quinn and my dog, I wasn't surprised by her breakdowns, Cherry and Quinn had been so cute together, but Quinn made big baby messes while Cherry just had to be let out and fed. I didn't leave her house until I made sure Nova ate at least one full baseball shaped cronut. I had one too, stress-eating used to be a part of my eating habits when I was growing up, and this felt like a good moment to stress-eat.

By the time I made it back to the apartment with Cherry, I noticed something off. I couldn't tell if it was because I hadn't been home in a few days or if it had been something else entirely. It was when I made it to my room that it all clicked, when I saw Lane standing in front of the bedroom window, he stared out like he was deprived of the city view below.

I could feel Lane's somber-depressed state the moment I widened the bedroom door. I walked in hoping he'd notice me, hoping he'd talk to me. There was something deeper going on with him and I just knew he needed to talk over it, with me more than anyone it seemed. I hardly found the energy to say anything to him, after being so upset from him leaving his family to seeing him like this. The room had been tampered by his emotions, causing me to feel whatever grief and darkness he felt.

"How am I supposed to do this, Kallie? How am I supposed to be a good dad to not one, but two babies? Quinn is barely a year old and soon, I'll have to do all the newborn stuff with Nova all over again." Lane paused just to turn and look at me, "I can't even take care of myself. My team needs me and I've been so laser focused on Quinn and Nova that it's taken a backseat. And now–"

"Now what? Your family comes first, Lane. No one expects you to know all the answers, but you leaving Nova is the biggest mistake you could make."

"I didn't leave." He said with eyes full of tears, he blinked them away, "I just needed a couple nights of quiet, to hear what my head and my heart are trying to tell me."

I took a step closer to my brother, "Yeah, and what did they say?" I tried to entertain his thoughts, just to get him to let it all out to me.

"My head is telling me to give up the game, Kal. I can't find a way around it. I can't find a way to be a good captain and husband and dad. It's too hard."

"That's not true." I answered, taking a step towards him, "Coach Guntz did it with Nova, that should give you hope that you can do it too."

"I just –" Lane shook his head, "I don't want to screw up my kids, I don't want to lead the team to losses and I… I don't want you to end up back in North Carolina, I don't want to see you go down another bad path."

I gave my brother a light smile, "I'm not going anywhere, if that helps you at all. And you're not going to screw up your kids, because you are going to be there. You are not going to be like our birth parents, you're not even close to being the kind of fathers we grew up with. So that needs to get out of your head, Lane. You have everything, literally." I almost chuckled, "You have a team that cares about you, a wife that loves you, a baby that dotes on you, and a full ass man that calls you his best friend."

Lane scoffed, "Jake and I are *not* best friends anymore, he made that pretty clear."

I almost gasped at his words, knowing that was hard to believe. Whatever happened between Jake and Lane should stay between them, but hearing my brother so upset over whatever Jake said made me want to press further.

"I don't want to get in the middle of you two, so if it's about me, I'll back off Jake. But if it's not… Jake is a really good guy. He's really turned himself around, he barely drinks anymore and –" I paused trying to think of what else I can say that wouldn't make it seem like I knew Jake better than Lane did, "Jake has just done a lot of really good things. I don't think whatever he said to you was meant for you to cut him out completely. He may have just wanted you to hear what he had to say."

Lane looked at me with a gleam in his hazel eyes, "I heard him. Loud and clear. He was right though, about almost everything. I look at you and see how much you've changed since you've been here, and listening to you now, it's like you can handle your own. I was always worried about you having the same experiences here since the guys in Florida aren't much better than in N.C. I just want to protect you and make sure that nothing can get to you again."

"I appreciate that, Lane. And I understand your reasons, especially if this is something you've been grappling with, but I'm an adult now. I have been for a while, and I know how to defend myself and hold my ground. I had a big brother to teach me that."

Lane smiled and I felt the room lighten around us, "I'm sorry if I startled you when you got home. I just didn't have anywhere else to go, and I wasn't going to actually skip town or get a hotel room. That would've made things worse."

"Yeah." I said with a sarcastic scoff, "I think you owe your wife a bigger apology. She's been a mess for three days. Madison couldn't even get her to sleep, and when I went over today, Nova and Quinn had been crying every five seconds."

"Shit. I really fucked up."

"No, you didn't. You just scared the shit out of her, so you need to go home and do your groveling and get your wife to sleep."

Lane smirked as he gave me a look. It took me half a second to have realized what he's thinking.

"Ew, gross. That is not what I meant! Please get your stuff and get out of here before I call the cops on your ass."

"I'll get out of here, but I do want you to know that I did a big brother thing while you were gone. I put the lease for the apartment in your name, so now you can do what you want with it. It's officially yours, for real."

The tears that fill my eyes only stop when they flew out of me as I gave my brother a big hug. I never expected Lane to do something so selfless but he's always been the kind of brother that does things for the right reasons and I just knew he'll be an even better dad to those kids of his.

Not even a full day later I surprised Jake at his apartment, I had only been to his place a handful of times compared to the crazy amount of times he'd been at mine. My apartment was just cozier, I guessed, plus Jake never wanted me to go back and forth with the dog. When I got there, Jake was not only surprised but wore only a towel. It had been perfect since the gift I had for him was something I had been unable to do the last few times we'd been together.

"Princess? What a delightful surprise." Jake said with a smile that made me melt. I couldn't even stop the smile from growing on my face when he invited me inside by pulling me in by my waist and kissing me until he had me pinned against his living room wall.

"What's the reason for this visit?" He asked, as his lips trail down my neck.

"Oh you know, the normal stuff." I teased.

"No, please tell me more." Jake teased back as he kissed my chin before taking my lips in his.

I bit his bottom lip as we part, "A thank you gift, for all that you've done – and said." I answered as he and I settled down. My feet finally met the floor after he had me and my body pinned to the wall.

Jake backed up to check me out, at least that's what it looked like as I see his cock pulse when his eyes dipped to my chest and lips.

"I never got the chance to give you a gift. You've given me such sweet and thoughtful gifts, and some not so sweet and naughty ones too. So I thought I'd give you one that fits all of those requirements."

"Well I'm not one to deny my Princess from giving me anything, but I'm sure it can wait so I can give you the kind of gift that just keeps you wanting more." Jake said with a wink as I pulled him closer.

"I'm sure there's plenty of time for that, but mine needs to come first." I replied, tugging on the towel around his waist. I looked down at his abs and his erection before I completely undo the tucked corner for him to be completely bare to me for once.

"Little Devil," He whispered, while pulling my chin up for me to meet his eyes, "Do you even know how to handle this?" I felt his dick rub against my thigh and it just made me want him more. That feeling in between my legs was my pussy aching for him but I promised myself he deserved more than just a ride.

"I do, because you taught me." I said as I got on my knees, Jake's hand stayed on my chin as I gazed up at him, "And this is something I've wanted to do for a while. So I hope my mouth as a gift is enough for you."

"Every part of you is more than enough for me, Princess." Jake whispered before I take my first lick. I heard his gasp as his grip on my chin lightens. I looked up at him as I licked the ridge of his cock, as I tasted his piercings on my tongue. I watched his expressions as I opened my mouth wide enough to take his tip in, as I took more and more of his cock into my mouth, until I couldn't anymore. It felt like the time I saw him in the mirror as he enjoyed me from below watching my every movement from the reflection.

"You're so perfect, Kallie." He said stroking my jaw as I sucked him, feeling the grip of his piercings in my mouth. It wasn't until I wrapped my hand around his cock that the sounds from my mouth are the only noise around us besides the occasional moan from his throat. I took him as deep as my throat allowed until I gagged, but it's the sound of his groan that kept me going, with my hand stroked him as my tongue and mouth worked his dick. Jake's hand feels the hollow of my cheek as I sucked him, just able to breathe through my nose, as his hand snakes in my hair and makes my head follow the same motion as my hand stroking him. I did it until I felt him thrust his cock more. My eyes looked up at my green eyed man, the handsome blonde locks as they fall in his face, the tattoos that run down his arms, the toothless grin that took over his face as I spat more of my saliva on his dick and sucked him harder and faster. Jake inhaled in a breath as his eyes shut tightly, his brows creased as I felt him stiffen and writhe beneath me until I feel him. Jake's cum shoot into my mouth, just that alone makes my pussy drip with wet desire for him.

Jake offered his hand as he helped me stand up, and as I swallowed every drop of his cum, he kissed me with more force than ever before. I wrapped my arms and legs around him, like I would a tree as he walked me to his bed, dropping me on his mattress just to shed my clothes.

"Fuck Kallie, I can't wait any longer." He whispered as his hands wrapped around my thong and ripped it.

"Jake!"

He hushed me, "You won't be needing underwear while you're under my roof." Jake took a long lick of me, "This pussy belongs to me here," He said before pressing his tongue deep into my pussy. "You belong to me just like that mouth belongs to my dick." He licked me again before he came up to look me in the eyes, "Got that, Princess?"

I nodded as I whispered, "Yes, Jake."

"Good," Jake said as he grabbed my throat and kissed me deep. I moaned as I felt the tip of his dick grind inside of me, "Now lay back and let me fuck you like the princess you are." The deep voice of his made the weight of his words fall into the deep recesses of my thoughts as Jake leaves marks of his lips all over my body. Kissing and sucking my nipples, leaving hickeys down my stomach and thighs until his tongue fucked me like he's been deprived of me too long. Jake didn't stop until I came all over his face, and even then I know it's not over when he fingers me, adding a third finger to stretch me for his cock.

I felt the tip of him slide inside of me, his piercings acting as a grip and extra pleasure the deeper he goes. I moaned when he pushed all of him inside of me. I'm hardly able to form words when he rigorously thrusted into me. His dick is so intoxicating the more he pumps inside me, the faster he got the more I wanted him deeper. Jake's hands held mine in place while he fucked me senseless. I felt my orgasm build and peak at the top as his hands dropped to my nipples and twist gently. It's when his fingertips trailed lightly across my clit that I came so violently that I saw stars.

Jake only let me rest for a moment before he's begging for more, his tongue back to fucking my pussy like his dick wasn't just there. I squirmed and gripped my legs around his head as he made me come again and again. He's not done with me yet, when he licked his tongue up my body until our tongues are fused together. Jake's cock reentered me easier the next time when he flipped us over and I ride him. His hands helped me bounce up and down on his cock as his piercings grip and hold onto me like a perfect fitting puzzle piece. My body writhes as I felt another orgasm build inside me, as he played with my clit as I continued to straddle and fuck him until I feel the top of my climax, and the beginning of Jake's cum shot into me, warm and full.

Jake gave me a chance to rest on his bed as he got up to get me a damp towel to clean up with.

"What do you think about you and I taking a bath?" Jake asked as he fell back on the bed next to me.

"How about you make that a steamy bubble bath and then I'll consider it." I answered, as I rested my head on my arm and stared back at him.

"Only for you, Princess." He said with a kiss.

Chapter 16

Jake

After Kallie gave me her *gift*, things between us had been changing. She had left things at my place, I was leaving things at hers, and well, it felt like our relationship had changed. No longer did I feel like just a friend, not even did I feel like we were still friends with benefits, no this felt. This was deeper. I had fallen, I had fallen so hard for Kallie I couldn't even recount the last time I felt like she wasn't mine. Maybe it was the season, the season of falling in love, the season of cuddling and fucking, or the season of changing a Facebook relationship status. Whatever it had been, I felt it, I knew she had to have felt it too.

Kallie hadn't gone on a date in months, she'd never even open her dating app when she'd get a notification. Hell, the only time she opened her phone was to take a photo of Cherry or to non-directly tell me she wanted me to fuck her again. It wasn't even a game anymore, there had been no reason to keep the charade of the benefits going. We even walked into work together, sure we kept the kissing and fucking between a locked office door and that one time in the locker room showers, but we were an *us*.

All I needed to hear was that she wanted it too, that Kallie wanted more. I had already felt like I put one-hundred percent of me into her, both literally and figuratively, I just needed her to catch up to feel and put the same energy with me.

It's when I ran into Lane that I felt the tug of regret. I had said some pretty heavy and rude things to him. I had been a grade A jerk to the guy and I wasn't sure anything I said would fix it. Kallie had told me what happened to him when we were on the camping trip, but ever since, I felt like it had all been my fault. I had ripped into him so good that I threw him down that depressive hole. I was only grateful that it was my princess, Kallie who got him out of it. She always would with that optimistic smile she had.

After I told Kallie about my parents on their death date she consoled me for hours, she tried her best to remind me of the good memories. And after only mentioning my grandpa once to her, she never stopped asking how he was doing. Every time the nursing home called me, she was always quick to ask if I was okay. Kallie definitely had no idea what she was doing to me every time she cared so much to ask. She was the only thing that kept me from breaking...

It took Lane and I not talking for two days that I finally couldn't take it anymore. I never ever talked to him like I had before, the guilt was spilling. I wasn't me without my best friend. And what was worse, the secrets I kept from him I still couldn't even tell. Not until I had talked to Kallie.

"Lane." I said, as he walked next to me down the hallway to the lockers.

Lane nodded back without a word as he continued to walk in silence.

"I'm not saying hey, I'm trying to talk to you." I pulled his arm to get him to look at me.

"You told me we weren't friends. So I'm sorry I don't want to talk, I just want to play the game."

"Well fuck the game for a minute, dude." I watched as Lane looked over at the locker room doors, close enough for him to run from me, but not close enough without me tackling him.

"What do you want?" Lane asked with a grind of his teeth.

"I owe you an apology. I said some things in the heat of the moment that I didn't mean."

"Oh, did you? I think you meant every word."

"You're right," I swallowed, "I meant some of the things I said, but that doesn't mean I meant all of it."

"Convincing." Lane replied with a cross of his arms. He just looked more pissed the longer he stood there with his copper eyes on me with his baseball cap creating an evil shadow of his brows.

"I'm sorry, Cap. I don't know what else to say, except I certainly didn't mean to end a near eight year friendship. I don't want to lose my only best friend. I know what I said, but that's never what I meant to say."

Lane sighed and let out a choke of a laugh as he shook his head, "Dude. We are so fucked up."

My brows creased, as my head cocked to the side, "We are?"

"Look at us. We're arguing and making up like Nova and Lexi. Literally we've turned ourselves into women over one stupid fight."

I chuckled, "Holy fuck, you're right."

"No shit, Sherlock."

I shook my head as I looked away to smile. I knew our friendship has been ridiculous, but I'm glad I could make up with the one person that's helped me out in more ways than one.

"Courtesy backpack ride to make it up to me?" Lane asked with a smirk.

I nodded, "Uh huh, yeah. Got to fix our friendship the same way we started it, right?"

"With me riding bitch on the back of your bike. Hell yeah." Lane said as we bumped fists.

"Yeah, but after I show you how to fucking hit a real home run." I teased as he and I sprinted for the lockers.

Chapter 17

Kallie

Jake texted me after work letting me know he'd be out with Lane for the night. It had been a few hours since I saw him last but I already missed him. I missed him like he was mine to miss. A weird feeling washed over me then, like I needed him to know that I belonged to him. I went through my pictures to find his tramp stamp, his cherub tattoo, also known as the mascot for our team, his team. It had proved to me time and time again that he'd been my angel in disguise.

I sent the pic to his phone, telling him that, that he's the angel that helped me from falling. It had been cheesy as hell, but he had to understand by now that I was in love with him. I was so in love with him that I was chasing just the idea of telling him.

"So I'm your angel and you're my Little Devil?" Jake responded in a voice note.

"Wouldn't want it any other way." I sent a voice message back.

"God, you're perfect, I hope you know that." His voice sounded so good, even when it was softened by the mic in his helmet. It's either that or I was just so stupid and so feet first in love with him that he just made me feel everything.

Jake and I texted a few more voice notes until I don't hear from him for a few hours. I tried not to think about him too much when he has his guy night with Lane. It's so bad that I actually go and hang out with Madison at her cafe to pass the time. I stayed out even later with her when she invited me to her usual hangout spot, a cute pub a few blocks away from her cafe.

By the time Madison and Hayes walked me back to my car it was way after one in the morning. My phone had died halfway through the night, after taking pictures of the pub and checking my messages for anything from Jake, I plugged it in and let it charge in the car on my way home. I'd never been much of a drinker, and certain drinks were triggers for me, it was enough to keep me away from ever getting drunk yet alone drinking one full glass of wine from the pub. I felt pretty good getting behind the wheel even late at night, but as I drove, I felt antsy.

I didn't know when my phone turned on but whenever it happened, a few minutes later, my phone lit up with a message. A voicemail from Jake got me all excited. I pressed a button and listened to the voicemail left by Jake, I assumed it had been a drunk call, but the longer I listened to the sound of it. The sound of the motorcycle, the sound of my brother yelling and a crash, was when I finally pulled off to the side of the road.

Very few cars beeped their horns as they passed me on the freeway, but I couldn't stop re-listening to the message. I couldn't stop the tears. I couldn't stop replaying the sound on my car's speakers, letting it loudly blare into my ears. I was shaking, my hands were shaking. My body felt cold as I turned off the car and walked out into a humid Florida night.

I ran to the other side of the road, where there was a sidewalk, hoping to find any sign of an accident on the main road. It had to be here, they had to have been, to go from a bar back to anyone's home, the freeway was the most common and populated area for any sort of accident...

Please don't be Jake's bike, I said to myself as I passed an abandoned motorcycle, with the sky dark blue it made it hard to see if the bike was Jake's. I pulled off to the shoulder of the road and hoped to god it wasn't him. Not a lot of people would have pulled over to help a stranger so I hoped what I'm doing wasn't going to bite me in the ass. As soon as I got out of the car and started walking I noticed a body near the trees and shrubbery. I ran to inspect the person with the black helmet, it was not Jake's helmet but helping whoever it was had become a part of my plan.

"Hey. Wake up. Please, wake up." I said to the body, they didn't jolt awake until my hands briefly touched their arms.

"Oh whoa. Holy shit." They said with their voice muffled by the helmet.

"Hey, no sudden movements." I tried to keep the guy down, as he tried to help himself up. "You might be banged up."

"We got run off the road by a couple of idiot drivers, didn't think we got hit but must've hit a bump or something."

"We?"

"Ugh, yeah." The guy took off his helmet and I'm surprised when I see my brother's face. Lane's face managed to look perfect for just being out a second ago.

"Lane?!" I almost screeched his name. "Was Jake with you?"

He looked at me with a confused look, "yeah, he was my backpack. I was testing out his bike to see if it would be worth upgrading mine."

"You– I–" I had no words as my eyes grew wide, my soon-to-be boyfriend was missing and my brother didn't even know it.

"What??"

"We need to look for Jake!" I yelled, starting before Lane caught up to me.

Both of us were screaming his name on the side of the road.

"So he said that you two are becoming close friends. You tell me if he gets too annoying, I can get rid of him if you want."

"Where is he, Lane?" I asked, not fully comprehending what he's said.

"He should be here." My brother's voice sounded a little slurred, as I turned to look at him my eyes followed his body fall into the grass. I ran to him and checked his breathing like I taught myself when my parents were back on drugs. He was just passed out. I assumed it was from the adrenaline of their crash but I couldn't help him or Jake when they were not together. I picked up my phone and called Nova.

Once my conversation with Nova came to an end, I was back on the hunt for Jake. Nova was on her way for her husband, while I continued searching for the idiot who let my brother ride a bike. The trust the two of them had in each other was idiotic when Lane was notoriously known for crashing bikes.

135

"JAKE!" I shouted again, the sky only turns darker the longer I searched but as I came up to the abandoned bike I noticed shoes just barely sticking out of another patch of shrubbery. I wanted to scream with the amount of feelings that ran through me, instead, I grabbed the feet and pulled just barely getting Jake out. As soon as I saw the helmet I knew it was him, I put up his visor, the sound of it clicking, as his eyes blinked awake.

"Little devil? Is that really you?" His voice rasped under the helmet. I helped him pull it off, noticing no pain that laced his breaths as he pulled the protective mask off his face. Jake's eyes looked a little red but it was the only part of him that looked injured.

"Are you okay? Please, Jake, tell me you're okay."

The little smile that split across his face made it better, "Of course I am, I'm just a little shaken. Come here." His hand wrapped around the back of my neck to pull me down. Our lips crashed together as I felt myself shake under him.

"What the fuck am I witnessing?" Lane's voice called out to us just as our lips separate.

I focused on Jake, "I was so scared I lost you."

"You could never lose me, Little Devil, I'm your Angel remember?"

"Hello?" My brother called out to us.

"You can't leave me now that my brother knows."

"Like there was a chance I'd ever not be by your side." Jake's smirk told me all I needed to know, as I kissed him again.

"Am I talking to a wall? Is this some sort of nightmare? Please, God tell me I'm not seeing my best friend and my sister kissing!"

The moment my lips parted from Jake's he asked me to help him up.

"Yeah, so we're together." Jake said directly to Lane.

"Jake! What are you–" I started but Lane extended his hand out as his way to silence me, it only worked because even Jake looked over at me for a split second before he continued.

"It's more than just sex. I know you had this hands-off rule, but your sister is actually her own person who can make her own decisions. She chose me. And I love her for it. No one's ever trusted me the way she does and if I'm honest with you, I trust her with my life more than I do you. I mean, hell, do you *see* where we are right now?"

"What the fuck, Jake?" Lane asked right before he tackled him to the ground. God, no. I quickly grabbed my brother and nearly fought him off of Jake, especially when I saw Lane raise his fist at him.

"No, no, no. Please don't do this, Lane." I said holding part of my brother and his fist, both from behind him, I was unable to see Lane's reaction. Instead, I just saw Jake's eyes go wide.

"Let him go, Little Devil. It's okay, just let him go." Jake's head nodded up and down as I felt tears spring loose from my eyes. His voice sounded shaky, but I'd never seen Jake look so confident. I lightly let go of my brother and backed away slowly.

"Punch me, Lane."

"Do you love her?" Lane's question held the air. I don't have a good look at either of them. I felt the beat of my heart go faster than it ever has on the back of Jake's bike.

Chapter 18

Jake

"Do you love her?" Lane's question hung in the air, but so did his fist. However I answered, it would look like I'm answering either in fear or as a lie.

"Drop your fist and I'll answer you."

"Why does that matter? God dammit Jake! Tell me right fucking now!" Lane yelled, with his hand gripped onto my shirt, like he was ready to land the biggest sucker punch across my face.

"Put your fist down first!" My voice shook.

"Answer me!"

"Fist first!"

"Dammit!" Lane yelled again, before punching. I winced expecting the blow, but it never came. Instead, I hear Lane scream before I felt the weight of his body come off of me.

"Lane!" Kallie's voice trickled off, almost like she's followed him. Then the sound of an ambulance rang in the distance. I closed my eyes for a moment before the sound blared in my ears.

I get up hoping I could see them but in the time it took me, a car pulled over behind me. Whatever PTSD in me, caused me to jump at the car's closeness, but the car shut off and that was when I immediately saw Nova.

"Where the fuck is my husband? What the fuck did you do this time, Jake??"

"Nova, I swear I didn't do anything! He was the one driving the thing. We swerved to avoid getting hit and then we fell into the side of the road."

"That's such bullshit. I'm furious that you let him ride that thing, you know he's banned since the last time."

"I know. He said he needed to blow off steam, I thought if I was his backpack we'd have more control and–"

"How'd that work for you?" Nova bit back.

"I'm sorry Nova. Truly." I watched her walk away to catch up to where I barely saw Lane and Kallie. I didn't know whether to stay away or follow. I was not really a part of their family, it felt like they might need a moment to themselves, or at least a moment alone with Kallie... Perhaps I should've always kept my distance from her, I should've known. Being alone was easier.

"Jake!" My Little Devil's voice shouted out. The feeling of loneliness dissipated as I nearly ran to her. Kallie was quick to wrap an arm around me, as I looked down at Lane and his hand.

"Is it broken?" The words dripped from my lips before I even think straight. Lane looked at me like he still wanted to punch me. Kallie holding onto me didn't help. I tried to pull away from her but it seemed to cause a stir in my stomach, especially when Kallie turned to look at me.

"Probably just sprained, but definitely swollen." Nova said comforting her husband.

"What's the matter with you?" Kallie asked me with a turn in her brows. I knew she and Lane weren't blood-relatives but the look on her face was almost identical to a similar expression of Lane's.

"Um. I feel like I should get out of here." I took steps away as I tried to gain distance between us but also so her brother didn't hear me.

"What? You're not serious, right? You just got into a pretty serious accident."

"Kallie, your brother wants to kill me. He nearly broke his hand to calm himself down. You don't think that what we're doing is – I don't know, not worth this?" I asked, trying not to sound as scared as I was, trying not to sound as alone as I felt.

I watched Kallie's shoulders drop, "And what are we doing?"

I looked away from her, "Come on, we never agreed to anything more. Things between us just escalated. I mean, I never expected you to come to my rescue on the side of the road."

"You– You think I wanted to find you like this? After our texts?! And I bet you think I came out here just to do this?"

"No, of course not. I'm just saying maybe it would be better –" I started.

"It would be better." Kallie finished in a quick breath.

"What? You don't even know what I was going to say."

"You were going to say it'd be better if we stopped this, right? Am I wrong?" Kallie asked as she crossed her arms over her chest.

I couldn't help but look at her, she had come so far from where she started and I was so proud of her. My Little Devil had done something I hadn't been able to do and that was standing up to me, I hadn't been able to look at myself in the mirror quite the way she was looking at me right now.

"Am I?" Her voice shook, as if she was overthinking her question, as if the quiet pause from me meant something else to her.

"You're not wrong." I answered, as I kept my voice steady, though it killed me that I wasn't saying something else.

I noticed as Kallie took a breath and swallowed, "Good. Then this is done."

"Kallie–"

"No. Let's not get– let's not talk. We don't ever have to talk about this ever again. What happened was– well you know. I appreciate what you did for me, but –"

"But you're done with me." I finished her sentence for her, "You'll find better."

Kallie didn't say anything else, just turned and walked back to her brother. I didn't find bother to look where she threw my mask, instead, I picked up my helmet and quickly put it on. I didn't even fully assess the damage of my motorcycle, I just pulled it up off the grass and used the key to see if it would start. My bike sputtered at first, but the second time it came to life and I sat on the bike. I should've tested it before I drove off, but I took the risk anyway. I just lost the one thing that made me feel human, my mortality had always been linked to my bike, and maybe it should stay that way.

Chapter 19

Kallie

After everything that happened between me and Jake, I didn't know what to feel. It'd been two weeks and I'd tried dating, I'd tried fucking someone else, but nothing. None of it felt like it did with him. I never believed in happily ever after's, but for a moment, with Jake, I did. Now I felt like a broken shell. I didn't feel like a princess or a devil, I felt like the ghost of a person I used to be.

My bedroom hadn't felt like mine, it felt like the remnants of a woman who discovered her body and of the man that fed her affirmations like he was a pastor that came to worship her. I couldn't even look at my kitchen countertops without being reminded of the first time he made me come. How was I supposed to live in the apartment without him? How was I supposed to love anyone else?

At work it was easy to play pretend, everyone already knew my fake smile. Everyone knew my positive and optimistic tone of voice like I was always happy and cheerful. And yet every day I had to see Jake's bike, the mirror still torn off the right side, the handle just scratched up, along with scratched up paint. Almost every day I saw Jake walk with his tight sleeved shirt and pants. Every day I walked into Nova's office, which had recently become my own, and I imagined the way I spread on my desk for the man as he fucked me while his team practiced from outside the window.

It felt like North Carolina all over again. Like I couldn't breathe, like I wasn't going to be able to live in the same space without him. And like everything was going to fall apart.

Chapter 20

Jake

Two weeks, two whole weeks without Kallie. My Princess, my Little Devil had her break from me. Two weeks and it nearly killed me, every time I walked by the office, the private room with her name on it, every practice I imagined her looking from her window looking down at me. My apartment felt the same, every bit of space had a memory of me making her come. The entire two weeks were torturous, a feeling I had never related to before.

I imagined this was how Kallie felt, that the pain was the same. How she dealt with it was beyond me, but I was not done, we were not over. She needed space, I gave it to her. Lane had needed space, so I gave it to him too. I wasn't giving up, I wasn't going to put either of us through that kind of pain any longer.

"So you told her you loved her, right?" My grandpa asked the second I walked into his room.

"No?" I said with a question in my voice, "How'd you know I loved her?" I sat down next to him at his computer. He let go of his mouse and looked at me, his eyes had a lifetime's worth of stories, but this expression was different from all the others.

"You're kidding, right? The second you started talking about this Kallie girl, I knew it was love." He said with his hand shaking towards me, "Your grandmother and I fell in love the same way."

I chuckled, "Like you couldn't stand the other until you had sex?"

"No!" He said with a smack to his desk, "The way she changed you and you changed her."

"She didn't *change* me, grandpa." I replied with a trill in my voice.

"Oh, right, because you were always a softy giving out puppies and helmets." My grandpa said with his eyebrows raised as his wrinkles deepen with the movement.

"Cherry isn't a puppy."

"My point is proven." With a finger raised he hushed me, "You know life doesn't get slower. You know the world won't be this way forever. You know death creeps up on everyone."

"Thanks for the pep talk, grandpa."

"Didn't I just hush you, boy?" Gramps said with an eye roll, "You never know when the last day is, is my point. I keep telling you to live in the moment, Jacob."

"I know, gramps. I've been living in the moment for a long time."

"You've been living in your bubble, not the moment. You ride that bike to escape the slow parts of life. You went out to bars to escape the fast parts. Kallie had you living right here, right in the now."

"You're talking out of your ass now." I stated, as I stood up, "I'm not here for help with Kallie, grandpa."

145

My grandpa followed my lead and tried to stand, though he held onto his desk the entire time, "No, you're here to tell me you're running after her because you love her, you just don't know how to tell her."

It's his words that get me to seriously look at him, "How'd you know that?"

"Your dad did it too. And let me tell you, you *don't* need a ring like he did. You need your best friend."

"What?"

"We ask for blessings not because we need them, but because the person you're with trusts them so much that they become a bigger part of them. Kallie's brother knows her better than she knows herself. That's why he told you no and not her. He has a part of her heart the same way she has a part of his, they might not be blood, but they're cut from the same cloth. They know what the hurt feels like and they try to help each other deal with it." My gramps explained with a knock on his desk.

"That's an interesting theory, gramps. I hope you know that I'm grateful for you." I said with a light hand on his shoulder.

"I know. I just try to help the idiots find their way home." He grinned. I took that as my cue to leave, I let a long silence pass between us as I gave him a light hug, but not before he grabbed my hand. "Paul." His voice changed when he used my dad's name, "Life will always find a way to hurt the best people, and when you're the best, you're always trying to lift up everyone else. Don't forget that the next time you think about helping that girl."

"You got it, dad." I smiled at him, hoping he didn't see the crack in my facade, not knowing enough about my parents' love story, but having heard that from my grandpa told me that my dad fought for my mom.

I left the assisted living home knowing full well I was not going to waste anymore time. I was not going to let my family, my person slip away from me without knowing the full truth. First, I had to follow my grandpa's advice.

I pulled up to Lane's house fully knowing he had nowhere else to go, I even had Hayes on standby if he tried to escape to the cafe or the field. I may have had Madison make sure that Nova kept Lane at home for the day, which might've been a risk, but I had to get him alone. I had to repair a friendship that was freshly taped up.

"Nope." Lane said, slamming the door in my face. What was up with this family slamming doors in my face?

I knocked again until Nova answered, "Hi, welcome to our home. We only let family and friends into our house and you're neither. So leave." She said as quickly as possible before slamming the door. This was going to be harder than expected.

Here was hoping the third knock did it. Lane answered again, this time stepping out and slamming the door so hard it broke off the frame. I tried not to chuckle nervously. I stepped back.

"How's the hand?" I tried to stay friendly.

"Broken." He showed off the cast around his wrist and up to his knuckles.

I bit my lip as I sucked in air, "That looks bad."

"Is there a reason you are harassing me right now?"

"I just need you to listen to me for at least a couple minutes." I heard the trill of my own voice.

"We're not doing apologies. This isn't something you can come back from with me."

"I love her, Lane. Like over the moon kind of shit. And I hate to say I planned it, but if I was going to fall in love with anyone, I'm glad it was your sister."

"What?" Lane quipped back.

"I get why now you didn't want me to be with her. It's because you knew she'd like me, because she's kind of like you. And I know that you didn't want me to hurt her, but she didn't give me a choice. I could've said anything that night and it wouldn't have mattered to her. She saw her big brother hurt and defending her. So she did what she had to, to protect you."

"As usual, Jake, you're wrong. If she wanted to be with you so much, she would have." Lane said with a blow following, "And the reason why she protected me is because I'm her family. I always will be, and you'll just be some stupid fuck boy who'll die on a bike."

I sighed and nodded, "You're probably right, but I'm going to keep telling you every day at every practice, at every game, at every event. I love Kallie. And I will fucking burn the world for her because deserves more, she deserves better."

"Jake, just stop!" Lane shouted. I pretended not to hear the footsteps coming from inside the house, but I knew it was Nova waiting to report back something to Kallie.

"I won't apologize for how I feel. I'm sorry that I have them, I'm sorry that it happened, but I'm not. I love Kallie. Remember when I said I wanted to find something like you and Nova? I did, I found it and I'm not going to stop until I can win her back and for some stupid reason she's loyal to her brother more than her own feelings. So if that means I have to tell you daily that I'm in love with her, I will."

Lane cocked his head to the side as he glared at me, "I have nothing else to say to you."

"I do," came a voice from behind him. I felt my heart drop at the sound of that voice.

"Go back inside." Lane said sternly to Kallie, but she pushed past him to come out to see me herself.

I finally got a good look at her for the first time in over two weeks. Kallie had cut her hair to her shoulders, she looked like she'd lost weight just by the way her chin quivered. And when I stared in her eyes, they're red rimmed as the aquamarine glitters with water. I watched her hands come together as she took a step toward me.

"I've never felt this way before." Kallie sputtered. "I thought," She rolled her eyes as she sniffled, "I thought this was just what everyone went through at some point."

"Kallie, it's more than that." I started to say with my hand outstretched towards her. Kallie took my hand in both of her hands.

"It is. You're right, because the last two weeks have been absolutely miserable. And as fun and crazy as we are together, I thought this was just a fling."

"As it was." Lane mumbled.

"It's not." Kallie stated looking back at him. She turned her head back to look ahead at me.

"Kallie, I love you so much and I'm so –"

"Don't you dare be sorry when I'm the one who did it, Jake." Kallie bit her bottom lip, "Am I still your princess?"

My lip quivered as I felt my heart dip, "You never stopped."

We pulled at each other as our lips came together in an unbreakable kiss. It's one I never wanted to forget, not as she gave me her tongue, not as I wrapped my hand around her neck and deepened the kiss more comfortably. When our lips parted, I felt lighter.

"I love you, Jake, with every part of me." Kallie saying those three words made it real, as everything around her seems to brighten. The sky didn't seem as dull, the expression on Lane's face almost looked—happy?

I kissed her again, "I'm never letting you go, Princess."

THE END.

Epilogue
Kallie - Nine Months Later

"Jake!" I yelled at him as he ran back over to me from the opposite side of the tattoo shop. He tried not to laugh as he leaned over to kiss me. "You know when I said you could pick out my first tattoo, I didn't think you'd be all secretive and make the tattoo artist not show me until after."

"I'm sorry, Princess. It's the only way for me to enjoy it." Jake said with another kiss. "Plus you already have your second one planned."

"Yeah, on my foot, with a picture of your ass, since that's where it always ends up!" The tattoo artist cracked up at my joke as he prepared the ink and his tattoo gun.

Jake's brows furrowed, "I thought it was going to be a little devil on your lower back?"

◻"Maybe," I answered, as I sat on the tattoo chair with my arms crossed.

◻"Come on, I thought you wanted to match your boyfriend with his lower back tattoo?" Jake said with a smirk.

◻"I can still make the cherub's hand look like it's not pointing at your ass crack." The tattoo artist interjected.

◻Both of us looked at him and said the same thing, "That's the best part!" Jake's tattoo artist carefully raised his hands like he didn't mean it. Meanwhile I kept forgetting that I was sitting in the chair, so his tattoo artist was soon to be mine as well.

◻"Did you pick a good placement?" Jake asked while he sat in a chair next to me.

◻"Yeah, I settled on my wrist." I answered, pointing to the spot on my left wrist. Jake nodded.

◻"Yeah, that's a pretty good spot, but I was thinking somewhere else." He said as he held the spot that I wanted to get tattooed.

◻"Of course you would, when you picked out the tattoo. Where else should I get it?" I asked as I made an aggravated snarl.

◻"Well, here, if you say yes." Jake sighed as he gripped my finger.

◻"You want me to get my ring finger tattooed? That's a pretty small tattoo for my first one, don't you think?" I asked with curved brows.

◻"Or just big enough." Jake shrugged as he pulled out a ring box from nowhere. "Since I've already committed a forever to you, I wanted to make it real."

◻I looked between him and the box with an open mouth, wide eyes and not a sound or word came out of me. He opened the box to show me a rose-gold ring with a princess cut opal diamond in the middle.

"I want to marry you in the realest way possible, simple or extravagant, it doesn't fucking matter, I just know I love you so fucking much and I can't wait a moment longer to make this official."

My tears didn't spill as I answered Jake, "Make it official. Tattoo a ring on me, tattoo your dick on me for all I care, it's the only one I want for the rest of my life." I pressed my mouth to his before he could even slide the ring on my finger. Jake had gotten me a million presents under the sun, but this was the one that topped them all, Cherry coming in second.

Epilogue
Jake - Three Months Later

□If a wedding had to be a disaster, I was glad it was ours. Cherry had run off the flower girl; Quinn laughed and ran back down the aisle in her pink floral dress, as Cherry barked and chased after her. Only half of the flowers were delivered and our officiant, Madison, had gone into preterm labor the night before.

□None of it really mattered once Kallie walked down the aisle in an ombre peony pink and purple wedding dress. Without an officiant it was just us reading our vows.

□"Jake, although I never thought our friendship would bloom in the way it did, I'm glad it was with you. Every day since I met you I think I loved you, maybe even more with each passing day. I couldn't imagine a life without you let alone five seconds. I'm so, so happy I'm marrying my favorite person, my best friend." Kallie finished with a tear.

▢Lane coughed from the side, "He's mine." I rolled my eyes at him as everyone that came to our little wedding giggled. I paid him no mind as I began.

▢"Kallie, if I've learned anything about my life, it's to never start a friendship with a plan. My plan had been to prove that I could be different. My plan wasn't about me falling in love with the girl of my dreams. All my days leading up to you were gray, were dull, and blah. But ever since I knew I loved you, colors started changing, food started tasting better, all to realize, it was because of you. I'd change nothing about who you are because it brought you to me, you brought me into a world full of light and color, and for that I am so grateful. And I am so ridiculously in love with you. And man, am I ready to upgrade your nickname, because you're more than a princess now, you're my fucking Queen." I finished up with the one thing that stopped me from almost sobbing in front of my friends and family. Kallie didn't even wait for the rings, instead she pulled me by my suit and kissed me.

▢Everything about our wedding felt right in that moment, nothing would ever top kissing her on our wedding day. In the same park I realized I loved her for the first time, where I now knew I'd be loving her for the rest of my life.

Acknowledgments

Wanted to take the time on here to shout out my favorite Instagram group chats that made this book happen...

Miles On Paper Indie Author Support Group.

The Smut Sluts Manor.

& Zaddy's Girls Channel (owned by zx10rzaddy).

Thanks to Zaddy (who I shouted out in this book) and his girl, Kait for the amazing pics that they let me use to make graphics for this book!

Thank you to all the friends that support me and read all my books!

And always shouting out Amanda for editing and so much more. I love and appreciate you so much!

We wouldn't be here without another amazing cover from my hubby, he's not reading this one... but thanks babe!

To my family that supports my book addiction and my creation of these books, thank you, I love you, but stop reading my books!

And to all my arc readers, street team, and the PAs that worked with me. YOU THE REAL MVPS!!!

Also by

Falling For The Angels Series

Coffee & Curveballs
Scoring & Scheming
Heartbreaks & Homeruns

Stand Alones
F*ck Happens